CW00524713

Natalie,

So great to meet
you at FBBF17!

Karlipe
xo

Books by Karli Perrin -

April Showers (April, #1)

April Fools (April, #2)

The Gift

Find Karli -

Twitter - @karli_uk

Goodreads.com/karliperrin

karlijperrin.blogspot.co.uk

karlijperrin@gmail.com

Dedication

To those who have a dream.

Never give up.

Acknowledgements

To April, my little guinea pig. What a journey this has been! Thank you for not giving up on me. No rain, no rainbow.

To Ivan. I couldn't have done this without you. Thank you for every single car journey where you have listened to me talk endlessly about April and her story.

To my parents. Thank you for creating me. Without you two, this book wouldn't exist! But seriously, thank you for everything that you do. Your support means the world to me.

To my brother. I miss the real We Say Summer. How about a reunion tour? All the cool kids are doing it these days.

To Emma. Thank you for designing my awesome cover. One day, karaoke will happen. And yes, we will be wearing double denim.

To all of my friends on twitter. Thank you for making me smile on a daily basis. I am so lucky to have 'met' you all. A special thank you to Zoe, Holly, Victoria, Courtney, Lisa, Yasemin, Natasha and Ally. You are the best cheerleaders a girl could ask for.

To all of the wonderful bloggers out there. Thank you so much, your support is invaluable to me. Sending high fives to you all!

And last but not least, to my readers. Thank you! I am so grateful for every single one of you. I hope you enjoy reading this book as much as I enjoyed writing it.

Are you ready? Here we go...

MANCHESTER EVENING NEWS

House fire leaves man in critical condition

A twenty year old man was left fighting for his life after a house fire in Manchester on Wednesday evening.

Lukas Roberts, a student at Manchester University, was found unconscious in the house on Wilmslow Road shortly after 6pm.

He was rescued by fire fighters and taken to Manchester Royal Infirmary where he is currently being treated for severe smoke inhalation and minor burns.

Witnesses claim to have heard Roberts shouting before using force to gain entry to the house. It has been confirmed that no other people were in the house at the time of the fire.

April Adams, the current tenant of the property, is believed to be a close friend of Roberts. She declined to comment at this time.

Police are treating the fire as suspicious and would like anybody with information to come forward immediately.

Prologue

I wiped away my tears as I stared at all of the different tubes and wires attached to Lukas's body. There were too many to count. The room was silent apart from the continuous beeping of the machines.

I edged closer to the bed and placed my hands on top of his, "I don't know if you can hear me but I need you to know that I'm sorry and I forgive you. We all make mistakes but that's human nature. Mistakes can be good for us, they teach us where we've gone wrong so that we can come closer to finding out what's right. I've learnt a lot these past few weeks and I know that you have too. What you did was brave and selfless and I will never be able to thank you enough. You need to hurry up and get better so I can at least try. I want my friend back."

I jumped when the door opened. Isaac stayed quiet for a moment before placing his hand on my shoulder, "Are you ready to go or do you need more time?"

I stood up, "I'm ready." I took one last look at Lukas before leaving the room.

I knew that deep down, he had heard every single word.

Chapter One

It had been two weeks since the fire.

Lukas was getting better.

Which meant that I was getting better.

Which meant that Isaac was getting better.

Isaac was my light in the darkness, the past two weeks would have been a total eclipse without him. I was staying at his apartment but knew that I couldn't for much longer. It was too risky in case anybody saw me going in or out. He still had over a week left to work at the University before we could act like a normal couple. Besides, I didn't know how much longer I could lie about staying at a hotel. Lucy, Hollie and even Dan had offered me a place to stay and Lucy in particular wouldn't let it drop. She had even brought a big bag of clothes to the hospital for me. I was grateful as all of my own clothes had been destroyed in the fire, along with everything else.

Lukas was lucky to be alive. The fire fighters had reached him just in time, any later and it could have been a completely different story. I shuddered at the thought.

The Police interviewed me several times after the fire. I told them that I had been out for a walk and was on my way home when Isaac stopped to offer me a lift. Isaac confirmed my story which eliminated us from being suspects. It felt wrong lying to them but the fire had still happened regardless of where I was or who I was with. They asked me a lot of questions about my relationship with Lukas and who might have a motive to set my house on fire. I couldn't think of anybody warped enough to do it but I did mention what had happened between Lukas and Madeline. I also told them about my disagreement with Abbie outside the coffee shop but I couldn't tell them the real reason why Abbie hated me.

I got chills when I thought about somebody intentionally setting my house on fire. What if I had been home at the time? Would it have been me lying in the hospital bed instead of Lukas?

Isaac pulled me into his arms, "Hey, where have you gone?"

I snuggled into his side, "I'm right here."

"What's on your mind?"

I linked my hand with his, "I was just thinking about the past couple of weeks. I don't know what I'd do without you."

"Well you'll never have to find out." He kissed my forehead, "I'd do anything for you."

I closed my eyes and let his words sink in. I knew how true they were. We stayed like that for a little while until my stomach rumbled.

Isaac laughed, "Hungry?"

"Apparently so." I looked at my watch and was shocked to see how late it was. I seemed to have lost all concept of time since the fire, "I don't even know what day it is."

He began to draw little circles in the palm of my hand, "It's Saturday, which means that we've got all day together tomorrow. No hospitals, no police stations, no insurance companies. Just me and you. One whole day to forget about all of the shitty things that have happened lately and just be happy."

I grinned, "That sounds perfect. I'm sorry for being such a mess recently."

"April, you don't need to apologise. You've had a lot to deal with. I'm so proud of how strong you've been but now that Lukas is getting better, it's time for you to start concentrating on yourself. Why don't I run you a bath and I'll order us a take-away?"

I nodded, "It's like you can read my mind, that's just what I need."

"I *can* read your mind. Right now you're thinking that I'm the sexiest man alive."

"Then you also know that I think you're the most arrogant too."

***

Fifteen minutes later, I was relaxing in Isaac's huge bathtub when there was a knock on the door. Instinctively, I looked down. Bubbles were covering most of my body. "Come in" I shouted. I was in no way prepared for what I saw when the door opened.

Isaac was standing in front of me completely naked. I gasped at the sight of him. He was absolute perfection. My eyes greedily roamed up and down his body, feasting on every inch of him. They stopped on his insanely toned abs for a few seconds before finally resting lower down on his erection. I was mesmerised. I wasn't exaggerating when I said that he was absolute perfection.

Every. Single. Part. Of. Him.

I instantly became the horniest person alive. Who needs a bath when I can bathe in Isaac's hotness? He slowly sauntered towards me wearing a cocky grin. He knew what he was doing to me, I was practically drooling.

"I have a problem" he growled. Whenever he's turned on, his voice drops an octave or two and turns all growly and husky. It's sexy as hell. He could probably make a ton of money working for some sex chat line. One word and ladies around the world would be dropping their knickers for him. He should come with some sort of Government health warning.

Highly addictive.

Take in small doses.

Causes high blood pressure.

I raised my eyebrow, "It doesn't look like you have a problem to me."

"Well I do. I have a *big* problem."

"It must be very hard for you" I joked, feeling like myself again.

"It is, it's ever growing. That's why I need your help."

I shrugged and tried to keep a straight face, "I'll try but I might *suck*."

He smirked but his eyes turned fiery. I knew what was about to happen. "Okay, I'll stop beating around the bush and just fill you in."

I nodded at him impressively and he grinned back at me. I loved playful Isaac. I also loved sexy Isaac. Combine the two and it drove me crazy.

"You said that a bath and something to eat is just what you *need*. Where do I feature in that equation?" He stepped into the bathtub at the opposite end to me. "I'm not impressed that my girl is content with a bath and a take-away. Actually, my ego's bruised."

My heart began to pound. He grabbed hold of my legs and parted them before sitting down between them. His eyes burned into mine, "I think you've forgotten what you *need*...what your body *needs*, so I'm here to remind you."

This was quite easily the most erotic moment of my life. His hands slowly trailed up my legs, sending electric shocks throughout my entire body. He began to caress my inner thighs before moving higher up to where I was aching for him.

He grinned, "God baby, you're so wet."

I couldn't help but laugh as I motioned to the water around us, "I'm completely drenched, can you see what you do to me?"

"Oh I can see it alright, I can feel it too."

I gasped as his fingers slid deep inside of me. He started off slowly, watching my reaction as he withdrew from me before entering again. My breathing hitched and my whole body screamed out for him.

"Is this what you need?" he asked.

I shook my head and watched as he raised his eyebrow in question. "I need more."

I didn't think that his eyes could get any more intense but I was proved wrong. "Tell me what you need."

"I need you inside me."

"But I'm already inside you" he replied, feigning innocence.

"I need your cock inside me right now."

"Well seeing as though you asked so nicely..." He kept his eyes fixed on mine as he completely filled me. "Fuck, you feel so good" he said before kissing me with such ferocity that it made my head spin. I bit his bottom lip while fisting a handful of his messy hair. "I've missed you" he said in between kisses.

"I've missed you too."

"I don't want to miss you ever again."

I moaned in delight when he took my nipple in his mouth and sucked hard. I could feel myself tightening around him as we picked up the pace. The water from the bathtub began splashing over the sides but we were too caught up in the moment to care. I forgot about everything else other than him.

"Is this what you need?" he asked.

"I need it harder."

"My pleasure" he said as he slammed into me. I was getting closer and closer to finding my release and the bathtub was getting closer and closer to being completely empty. He increased the pace and my whole body tensed up as I cried out his name. He slowed down until my body stopped shuddering underneath him. Taking my face in his hands, he pushed into me once more until he found his own release. He growled but kept his eyes locked onto mine. He kissed my forehead before pulling me into his arms. We stayed like that for a little while until he stood up and I was once again mesmerised by his body. I would never get used to seeing him in all of his glory.

"I think we need more towels" he announced.

I laughed and looked down at what little water remained in the tub, "I'm actually pretty dry."

He raised his eyebrow, "That's debatable. We'll try the shower tomorrow, I think it'll make less mess." I grinned as he passed me a towel. I stepped out of the tub and wrapped it around myself, pouting at him when he did the same. "Hey, I don't want the pizza delivery woman getting the wrong idea when I open the door."

"It's a woman?" I asked.

"Yeah, don't tell anyone but she throws in free potato wedges just for me."

I narrowed my eyes, "In that case, go and put some clothes on. A baggy jumper will do."

He winked at me before leaving the room. I smiled as I turned around and gazed into the mirror. It had been a rough couple of weeks but I was glad that I was still able to smile after everything that had happened. I scraped my long brown hair into a messy ponytail and wiped away my smudged mascara. I washed my face in the sink before drying it off. My eyes looked tired and not as blue as usual.

"See how beautiful you are?" Isaac asked as he came up behind me, wrapping his arms around my waist. He was now wearing a plain white T-shirt and grey sweatpants which were hanging dangerously low.

I blushed and looked away, "Thank you."

"You're even more beautiful when you blush."

I turned around so that I was facing him, "Are you purposely trying to make me swoon?"

"That depends, is it working?"

I laughed, "Yes."

"Then no, I'm not trying at all. It's all natural charm."

"Well be careful, you'll burn out at this rate."

"Baby, I could keep going all night long."

I raised my eyebrow, "I might have to test you on that one."

"We've got all day together tomorrow, just saying."

Before I could reply, there was a knock at the front door. Isaac licked his lips, "Mmmmm, the pizza's here." He kissed me on the forehead and turned to walk out.

"Isaac?"

"Yeah?" he asked, turning back around.

"Please don't make that sound in front of the poor pizza woman."

He chuckled before walking out.

Chapter Two

After stuffing our faces with pizza, we were relaxing on the sofa with a bottle of wine. I hadn't realised how hungry I had actually been.

"Can I ask you something?"

I smirked, "I don't need another bath...yet."

He laughed, "I'm only asking this because I'm trying to be responsible..."

"Go on."

"I know you're an intelligent girl but are you on the pill?"

"Oh, so now you want to be responsible? It's a little too late for that. No I'm not, I assumed that by not wearing a condom you wanted to be my baby daddy."

He grinned, "I do but I also want you to graduate and have a career first."

I cocked my head to one side, "Have you thought about this before?"

"I'm in love with you, of course I've thought about it. Any guy who denies it are liars or are with the wrong person."

I grinned like a complete idiot, "Well yes, I'm on the pill. Luckily, I carry them in my bag so they weren't destroyed in the fire."

"So mini Isaac's can wait for now."

"I don't know if the world could handle mini Isaac's."

"Hey, why not?"

"They would probably be heartbreakers just like their Dad."

His mouth fell open, "I don't break hearts! If anybody's a heartbreaker, then it's you."

"What did I do?"

"Look at you acting all innocent."

"I'm not acting, I *am* innocent."

"What about the stockroom?" he asked.

"What *about* the stockroom?" I shot back.

"Is that your idea of being innocent?"

"*You* kidnapped *me*, remember?"

"And *you* rubbed up against *my* leg, remember?" I rolled my eyes and he laughed, "That night was all your fault, you came in wearing a long white dress. What was I supposed to do?"

"What did my dress have to do with it?"

"You may as well have worn a veil to match. You're lucky I didn't kidnap you for real and take you to Vegas."

I narrowed my eyes, "So that's why you were so angry that night?"

"I wasn't angry, I was upset. Everything that I'd ever wanted was being flaunted in my face and I didn't know what to do. I thought that I'd lost you for good."

"Hence the kidnapping?"

"Hence the kidnapping. Desperate times call for desperate measures."

I laughed, "Even though you scared the shit out of me, I'm kind of glad I chose to wear that dress now."

"Because you know how much it tortured me?"

"No, because it led us to this moment."

He nodded, "That night was a turning point for me. When I looked into your eyes, I knew that I hadn't lost you."

My heart fluttered at how true his words were. *I* had been lost but Isaac never lost me, not once. "Eleven days" I whispered.

His eyes twinkled with emotion, "Eleven days" he repeated "...until I get to kiss the shit out of you in public."

"Oh no, are we going to be one of those annoying PDA couples?"

He nodded, "It's happening."

I rested my head against his chest and listened to his heartbeat. There was no place I would rather be.

Chapter Three

"Are we nearly there yet?" I asked for the hundredth time.

He grinned, "Are you trying to annoy me on purpose?"

"That depends, is it working?"

"Yes."

"Then yes, I'm doing it on purpose. I could never be this annoying unless I tried really, really hard."

"Well for the record, it was actually kind of cute the first fifteen times you asked."

I shrugged, "I wasn't even *trying* to be cute, that was all me."

He chuckled, "Of course it was. And the answer is yes, we're nearly there."

About ten minutes later, we turned down a road marked as private.

"It's okay if you're lost." I pointed to the sat nav, "I don't trust her, her voice is creepy."

He laughed, "You don't trust her because she's a woman."

I sighed dramatically, "Well what am I supposed to think? She's always following you around, telling you what to do. There's a word for people like her, you know."

"A girlfriend?"

I scowled at him, "Very funny. I was thinking more along the lines of a stalker."

"What's the difference?"

"Be careful, be very careful."

"We're here" he announced with a huge grin on his face.

"Stop trying to change the sub...wow." We pulled up in front of the most beautiful house. It had an all white exterior and a huge wooden door. "This place is beautiful."

"I thought you might like it, I used to come here when I was a kid." He switched the ignition off before jumping out and walking around to my side. He opened the door and reached out for my hand.

"Where are we?" I asked.

"Let's just say that I know the owner."

My eyes immediately darted to his, remembering the last time he used that line, "Wait, do you own this place?"

He laughed, "No, not this time. The owner is a family friend."

"Where are they now?"

"He's in New York. He said that I could come out here whenever I wanted so I decided to finally take him up on the offer."

"Well it's gorgeous."

"Wait until you see the inside."

***

Each room was more impressive than the last. Even though the exterior was traditional, the interior was modern and had quirky artwork and furniture. The downstairs was open plan and had the most amazing fireplace. I could picture us sitting in front of it, all cozy on a cold winters night.

"There's one more thing that I want to show you." He led me over to a wall made entirely of frosted glass. "This is my favourite part of the house." He pushed a button on the wall and the glass instantly turned clear. I gasped as I took in the breathtaking view.

We weren't just in a beautiful house. We were in a beautiful lake house. The lake was surrounded by trees, making it completely private. It was so perfect, it looked like a painting.

"Do you like it?"

"Like it? I love it! I want to live here."

"He was actually going to sell it a few months ago but I talked him out of it."

"Why would he want to sell this place?"

"He spends most of his time in New York these days." He took hold of my hand and led me outside. I was thankful that it was a dry, sunny day. We walked right up to the edge of the lake and as I looked out across the water, I felt the craziness of the past few weeks begin to float away.

"Fancy a swim?"

I raised my eyebrow, "I've not brought my swimming costume."

"Who said you need a swimming costume?"

"So you've brought me all this way just to go skinny dipping?"

He laughed, "Well it's bigger than the bathtub." I shook my head but couldn't stop myself from laughing. He nodded in the direction of a little rowing boat, "How about a compromise?"

"I would love to, I've never been in a rowing boat before." We began to make our way over to it when I saw a ripple in the water. "Wait, are there any creatures in there?"

He laughed, "Creatures?"

"Yeah, like crocodiles or snakes."

"No crocodiles, no snakes" he replied, trying his best not to laugh.

"So nothing that can bite me?"

"Just me, now come on." He stepped in before offering his hand to help me in. I squealed when it rocked, praying to god that I didn't fall in. Isaac laughed as I sat down very slowly. "You ready?" he asked. I nodded and he began to row.

I quickly became transfixed by the way his biceps moved with each stroke. The more I watched him, the more I wanted to go skinny dipping after all. "Thank you."

"What for?" he asked.

"For wearing a short sleeved T-shirt, rowing looks good on you. You should do it more often, probably topless next time."

He laughed, "I will if you will."

I grinned as I looked out across the lake, "This place really is beautiful."

"It's even more beautiful with you here."

He stopped rowing when we reached the middle of the lake.

"Do you need a rest?" I asked.

"Nah, I thought that you could take over."

"Oh, well I'll give it a go."

He took my hands in his, "I'm joking, I just want to enjoy this with you. I know you've been through a lot recently, you could have given up but you keep on fighting."

I looked down at our hands, "I remember the first football game of the season, not because we won but because of you. I remember the way my heart sped up when I saw you. I remember your face right before you walked away from me. I remember how numb I felt for days afterwards. I remember how you told me that you would fight for us. I let myself down that day and I won't let it happen again. Thank you for not giving up on me."

"I never had a choice when it came to you. I don't just want you, I need you."

He was right. As much as I had tried to fight it at first, I knew all along that my heart belonged to him.

"Do you remember how I told you that I had a difficult time after Sienna died?" I nodded. "Well I started to see a psychiatrist who told me to keep a diary. They said that it might help if I wrote my feelings down. It felt weird at first, how many men do you know who keep diaries?" His eyes turned sad, "But how many men do you know who have had to bury their little sister? So I tried it and it actually worked. I'd write in it whenever I felt angry or upset. Just like song writing, it gave me an outlet for my grief. As time went on, I started to write in it when I was feeling happy too. It made me feel like I was sharing things with my sister. I've carried on ever since, I guess it's just habit now. Can I share something with you?"

"Of course."

He smiled before retrieving something out of his pocket. He unfolded the piece of paper and began to read,

"I met a girl today. She was crazy. And funny. And sexy. And smart. And beautiful. I don't even know her name but I know how she made me feel - alive. She welcomed me to the twenty first century. Literally. She will never know how much I needed to hear those exact words. I've been living in the past but that's about to change."

He looked up from the paper, "I guess now you know."

I smiled, my eyes brimming with tears, "Now I know."

***

We spent the majority of the day in the bedroom. We also tested out Isaac's theory about the shower. He was right, it made a lot less mess than the bath. We decided to go home when it started to get dark, which wasn't very late now that it was October.

"Have you had a nice day?" he asked as we pulled away from the house.

"No." His head shot around so fast, I was surprised that he didn't give himself whiplash. I giggled, "I've had a perfect day."

He pretended to wipe his forehead, "Phew, you had me worried then."

After an hour of playing i-spy and the 'would you rather' game, his phone began to ring. It was linked up to the hands free in his car so it interrupted the quiet music that had been playing. He frowned, "It's my mum, do you mind?"

"Of course not."

He pressed a button to accept the call, "Hi Mum, is everything okay?"

"Hi sweetheart. Yes, everything's fine." I grinned when she called him sweetheart. "But I've just had a worrying call off Abbie."

My grin faded as Isaac immediately clicked the 'hold' button before putting in an ear piece. I narrowed my eyes at him, wondering why he didn't want me to hear the rest of the conversation. He pressed the hold button again before speaking, "Yes, I'm here. Carry on." A few seconds later, he shook his head, "That's not my problem. *She's* not my problem." He gripped the steering wheel tighter until his knuckles turned white, "What did she say word for word?" He took a deep breath and I watched his face flood with disappointment. "Don't worry, I'll take care of it. Bye."

I sat there quietly, waiting for him to say something. When it became clear that he wasn't going to, I couldn't wait any longer, "Is everything okay?"

"Mmmhmm."

"Why are you lying to me?"

"I'm not lying. Everything's okay, I can take care of it."

"Take care of what?"

"I'd rather not talk about it."

"Well I want to."

He turned to face me, "April, please trust me and just drop it."

"Why did you take your mum off speaker phone?"

He sighed, "Because I don't want to drag you into family shit."

"It didn't sound like *family* shit, it sounded like *Abbie* shit. Why did she call your mum?"

"Because she's being typical Abbie."

"Meaning?"

"Meaning I've been dealing with her childish behaviour for years. She's in trouble so she rang my mum knowing that I would help if my mum asked me to."

"What kind of trouble?"

He shifted in his seat, "I don't know, that's what I need to find out."

"Why can't you say no?"

"Because Abbie doesn't know the meaning of the word. You know what she's like, it's best to keep her on our side for now. Please just trust me on this one."

I turned to look out of the window as I spoke, "I trust *you*. It's Abbie who I don't trust."

Chapter Four

We drove the rest of the way in silence. I was relieved when we pulled up in the car park behind his place. He ran his hand through his messy hair and I noticed how he kept the engine running. He took hold of my hand and began to stroke it reassuringly, "I'll be back as soon as I can."

"Do you mean you're going to help her right now?"

I watched the muscles in his jaw tighten, "Yes."

"Can't it wait?"

He sighed, "No."

"Do I not get an invitation to her pity party?"

He frowned, "April..."

"I was joking, I'd rather stick pins in my eyeballs. Have fun." And with that, I got out of the car and didn't look back.

When I got inside the apartment, I waited until I heard his car drive away before taking a few deep breaths. I wasn't about to sit on my own and wait for him to return. I found my phone and text Lucy -

"Have you still got a spare room? x"

A few seconds later, she replied -

"Hell yes!"

I'd been planning on moving out of Isaac's when I started going back to class, which was tomorrow. One day early wasn't going to hurt.

"How does half an hour sound? x"

"It sounds awesome, see you soon."

I gathered my things together, which consisted of a bag of Lucy's clothes and my toiletries, before walking over to her place. It was about a fifteen minute walk, not too far from Lukas's house.

When I arrived, she opened the door and threw her arms around me. I was caught off guard but I think a hug was just what I needed. "That dress looks much better on you than it ever did on me, you can keep it. Come in."

Her place was only small but I liked it immediately. The orange and yellow decor gave it a warm and positive feel. She gave me a mini tour, saving the spare room until last. "And this is your room..." she said as she opened the door.

"It's hardly my room, I'll only be here for a couple of weeks until I sort everything out with student services."

"Well it'll be *your* room for a couple of weeks then."

It was nearly as big as my old bedroom. It had a single bed and some fitted wardrobes, even though I didn't have anything to hang in them apart from Lucy's clothes. I needed to go shopping. "Thanks Lucy, I really appreciate everything."

"No problem. It's going to be nice having someone else here with me, it can get lonely sometimes. Are you hungry?"

"I'm starving." Isaac had been planning on cooking but now he had more important things to take care of.

"I'll go and make us something to eat while you settle in."

"Thank you." I watched as she practically skipped out of the room. I sat down on the bed and looked out of the window just as my phone started to ring.

Isaac.

"Hello" I answered.

"Where are you?"

"Lucy's."

I heard him breathe a sigh of relief, "I was worried, I came home and you weren't here. It's getting late and you didn't text or leave a note. Your clothes were gone...I thought..."

"Thought what?" I asked when he trailed off.

"I don't know what I thought, I was just worried."

"Well I didn't mean to worry you, I just didn't know how long you were going to be."

"Are you coming back?"

"Not tonight. We've talked about this, I was going to move out tomorrow anyway."

"I know, I was just looking forward to spending one more night with you."

I bit my lip to stop myself from saying something that I might regret.

"Are you okay?" he asked.

"I'm fine."

"There's that awful word again."

"So what happened with Abbie?" I couldn't hold it in any longer.

He sighed, "I'll tell you...just not right now."

"Fine."

"I seriously hate that word."

I seriously hate that woman.

"Are you going to be okay going back to class tomorrow?" he asked.

"Of course."

"Well you know where I am if you need me or want to take some time out."

Lucy appeared in the doorway, "I made us omelettes, they're ready." When she noticed that I was on the phone, she mouthed sorry before hurrying off.

"Did you hear that?" I asked Isaac.

"Yes, omelettes, without me. Awesome."

"Stop sulking."

"Will you come and see me tomorrow night?"

"It depends how good Lucy is at spooning."

Chapter Five

My first day back after the fire wasn't as bad as expected.

It was worse.

A total number of seventeen people asked me about the fire.

Yes, I counted. Yes, I know it's sad.

I started off being polite but quickly lost my patience. By the end of the day, I think people were too scared to even come near me. I knew it wasn't their fault, they were just interested but I was tired of reliving what had happened.

I rang the one person who was guaranteed to cheer me up. "Hey Kitty, talk to me about something non-fire related."

"Okay, are you sitting down for this?"

"No, I'm walking back to Lucy's place."

"Well grab onto a lamppost or something because I have big news. I've lost my V card!"

I gasped, playing along with her, "Oh my god! Did it hurt?"

"Yep, I've never seen so much blood."

"How do you feel?"

"Different, more mature..."

"Well I'm waiting until I meet the right guy, I won't give in to peer pressure."

She laughed, "Were we really like that once upon a time?"

"Probably. So Ian's finally remembered how to use it?"

"Oh yes, the drought is over...literally."

"Too much information."

"What's wrong? Aren't you happy for me?"

"Of course I am, I'll send you a card in the post. So how did you crack him in the end?"

"The kinky bastard likes to be tied up. Who knew?"

"Wow, it's always the quiet ones."

"He's wasn't so quiet when I spanked him using a..."

"Changeeee of subject!" I shouted.

She laughed, "Okay, there's something that I've been meaning to ask you for a while now."

"Sounds serious?"

"It is. Were the fire fighters hot?"

"You did *not* just ask me that."

"I actually did. Lukas is getting better so I'm allowed to focus on other important things. So? Were they hot?"

"I wasn't really thinking about that at the time, believe it or not."

"Yeah, I guess you didn't need to when Isaac was standing next to you. Who needs fire fighters when you've got your own little hottie?" She began to sing *'Sex on fire' by Kings Of Leon.*

"Oh yeah, it had nothing to do with the fact that my house was on fire and my friend was trapped inside."

"Okay, okay. What about the policemen? Were they hot? Did they have handcuffs?" She giggled which was so infectious that I had to bite my lip to stop myself from laughing. She didn't need to be encouraged any further. "I'll take your silence as a yes."

"And on that note, it's time to go. I'll talk to you later."

"Wait...did you see their *batons*?"

"Bye Katie." I grinned as I ended the call, I knew that I could rely on my best friend to cheer me up. To keep my good mood going, I rang Isaac. I missed hearing his voice already.

He answered immediately which made me smile. "April, now's not a good time." He sounded stressed. It wasn't exactly the greeting that I had been hoping for.

"Oh, okay."

"Can I call you back later?"

"Yeah, is everything okay?"

"I'm just busy."

"Are you still at work?"

He hesitated before answering, "No."

"Oh, so where are you?"

"Why does it matter?"

I narrowed my eyes, "I was just wondering..."

"Look, please can you interrogate me later?"

"Please can you stop being a dick later?"

He sighed, "I haven't got time for this, I'll call you when I'm home."

"Whatever" I replied, which was universal girl code for 'fuck you'. I hung up before shoving my phone back in my pocket. So much for my good mood.

I replayed the conversation over and over again in my head. If he wasn't at work, where was he?

***

"How was your day?" Lucy asked as I walked through the door. I only had one class with her on a Monday so I hadn't seen her all afternoon.

I groaned, "Crap."

She patted the sofa, "Sit down. Vent."

I put my bag down and made my way over to her. "Fifty billion people asked me about the fire."

She raised her eyebrow, "Wow, that's a lot of people. You're really popular."

"I don't want to be popular, I just want to move on."

"The first day back is always the worst, it'll die down."

"I hope so."

"Anything else that you want to vent about?"

Yes. Isaac.

"Nah, how was your day?"

"Uneventful. I do have some news though."

"Spill."

"Lukas is home."

I sat up straighter, "He is?"

She nodded, "He got back this afternoon."

"That's great, how is he?"

"He sounded okay on the phone. I'm actually going to visit him, I was waiting for you to get back first to see if you wanted to come?"

My heart started beating faster, "Um, I'm not sure..."

"April, I think you two should talk. I'm sure there's a lot that needs to be said."

Lucy didn't know the half of it. As far as she was concerned, I hadn't spoken to Lukas since we broke up and he went to Paris.

"I think I should wait a little longer, give him some time to settle in."

"Don't you want to see how he is? He risked his life for you."

"I'm quite aware of that" I snapped.

"Sorry, I just realised how that sounded. I wasn't having a go at you but he must still have strong feelings for you to run into a burning building."

"I'm sure he would have done it regardless of whose house it was. Anyway, he might not want to see me."

"He does."

"Did he say so?"

She nodded. I closed my eyes and thought about how it might hurt Isaac's feelings if I went to see Lukas alone. But then I thought about how weird he had been acting on the phone. Me and Lukas were friends, it wasn't a big deal. Just like him and Abbie were friends. "Okay, I'll go."

She stood up, "Great, let's get going."

"Now? But I've only just got in."

"He's still sleeping a lot, we should go and see him now while he's awake."

Chapter Six

Ten minutes later, we were walking down Lukas's street. Lucy had talked the whole way there which had kept my mind preoccupied but when I saw a car similar to Isaac's drive past us, it made me question what I was about to do. Shouldn't I speak to Isaac first?

It was too late. As we walked up to his front door, memories from the last time I was here flooded through my mind. It was the night that we had slept together. So much had happened since then. Lucy knocked on the door before walking straight in, which made me raise my eyebrow in question. "He told me on the phone to come straight in."

I mentally told myself to stop being a baby as I stepped into his flat but I felt like crying when I saw him sitting on the sofa. He glanced at Lucy before his eyes locked with mine. We were silent for a long time. After what seemed like an eternity, Lucy cleared her throat, "I'm just going to make a quick phone call outside." It was obvious that she was giving us some privacy.

"Hi."

I smiled at the sound of his voice, "Hi."

"It's good to see you."

"It's good to see you too, I'm glad you're home." He smiled as I slowly walked over to the sofa and sat down beside him. I couldn't help but stare at the burn on his cheek. It would definitely leave a scar which meant that he would have a constant reminder of the fire. He would never be able to forget what happened that day. *I* would never be able to forget. I let out the breath that I was holding, "You scared me."

He placed his hand on top of mine and I felt the biggest surge of regret wash over me. If only I would have followed my heart from the start, none of this would have happened. I wouldn't have hurt Lukas, he wouldn't have hurt me and we would still be best friends. I didn't know if it was even possible to go back to being friends like we were in the beginning.

"You scared me too so that makes us even."

"It was horrible seeing you in the hospital."

He laughed but it turned into a chesty cough, "You're not doing much for my ego right now."

I smiled at the way he was trying to make light of a shitty situation. It was such a typical Lukas thing to do. "I hate seeing you sick, seeing you with burns."

"Again with the ego thing." He pulled down the sleeves on his T-shirt, hiding more burns on his arms. "Are there any other things that you hate about me while you're offloading?"

I laughed, "Yeah, you're such an attention seeker getting your name in the newspaper. I bet you have an agent now, Mr Big Time."

"I do, I'm actually writing a book about my traumatic experience."

I rolled my eyes, "That doesn't surprise me. What's it called?"

"I'm thinking about 'Fire in my heart'."

I had to laugh at that one, "I like it."

He nodded, "You can have a signed copy. And as far as the burns are concerned, they'll turn into scars soon and women dig scars."

"That's true, you do look pretty badass."

His eyes twinkled, "Thank you for coming to see me, I've missed you."

"Pfft, you were sleeping and getting crowded by hot nurses, I bet you didn't even think about me."

"You know that's a lie."

I did.

"April, I have a few things that I would like to get off my chest, if that's okay with you?" I nodded, preparing myself for what he was about to say. We were both quiet as I waited for him to speak. "The day of the fire was the worst day of my life. Not because of what happened to me but because I thought that I'd lost *you*. In that moment, when I thought that you were inside the house, all that mattered was getting you out of there. There was never a choice for me, I was always going inside. I know that you're a good person which means that you're going to try and blame yourself but no part of what happened was your fault. I would run into that house every single day for the rest of my life if it meant saving you from getting hurt. Although I regret how things ended between us, some selfish part of me doesn't regret anything because it led to something so real. Those moments that we shared had nothing to do with anybody or anything else. It didn't matter what had happened in my past or what was going to happen in our futures. All that mattered was us. I really hope that we can be friends again."

I couldn't stop the tears from falling, "I'm so sorry, I should have answered your phone calls, I should have told you that I wasn't at home."

"Stop it right now. What did I say about not blaming yourself? Look, I'm okay."

"How did you know about the fire?"

"I was walking home when I got a phone call from a friend. As soon as they told me about the fire, I ran. I ran and didn't stop until I got there. You weren't answering your phone so I went in. I have no regrets." He paused and looked down at his hands, "There's something that I need to ask you. It's okay if you don't want to answer but I would really appreciate it if you did." I nodded. "Are you in love with Isaac?"

My heart leapt at the mention of his name. Even though I knew that it was going to hurt him, I owed him the truth. "Yes."

"That's what I thought but I needed to hear it. The night before the fire, I saw the way that you looked at each other. I didn't want to believe it, it was easier for me to think that he must have taken advantage of you because you were upset. But I've had a lot of time to think recently and I want us to go back to being friends. I want to start over and earn your trust back. Above everything, I want you to be happy."

I let his words sink in as I remembered why I liked being around Lukas so much. He was a genuinely good person. Sometimes good people make bad choices but that doesn't make them bad people, it just proves that they're human. "Thank you."

"If Isaac makes you happy, then I'm happy. If Isaac makes you upset, then I'll be upset...and I'll kick his ass."

I laughed before he pulled me into one of his signature bear hugs. When I pulled away, I glanced down at my watch. "I think Lucy's been kidnapped."

"Well we'd better call Liam Neeson."

I smirked, "I deleted his number, his constant texts were starting to annoy me." I stood up and walked over to the front door before looking outside. Lucy was nowhere to be seen. I dialled her number and could hear music in the background when she answered. "Hey, where are you?"

"I'm at the pub with Dan."

"Oh, how did that happen?"

"I was sitting on the wall outside when I saw him walking down the street. I wanted to give you and Lukas some time alone so I persuaded him to come to the pub with me."

"I bet he didn't take much persuading."

"Nope, I told him that I'd buy him a drink and he was sold."

"When will you be back?"

"I'm not sure, I might stay here for a while. They're actually playing music that I like tonight. Why don't you come and join us?"

"No thanks, I'm just going to head back and have an early night. I'll see you tomorrow."

"Wait...are you and Lukas okay?"

"Yeah, we're good."

I walked back over to Lukas. "Do we need to go on a rescue mission?" he asked.

"Yes, we need to rescue her from Dan."

"Why is she with Dan?"

"They're at the pub."

He nodded in understanding, "Lucy took one for the team."

"We definitely owe her one. I think I'm going to head home, let you get some rest."

"You don't have to, you can stay if you want."

"I'm really tired." I grinned, "Some of us actually went to class today."

He laughed, "Some of us are too busy running into burning buildings. You know, saving people's lives."

I held my hands up as I began to back out of the room, "You win this time. I'll see you soon."

***

I spent the rest of the night debating whether I should call Isaac. When I was lying in bed at ten thirty with no phone call, I began to question why he still wasn't home. It was sometime around midnight when I finally fell asleep. I felt better after my conversation with Lukas but I couldn't shake the feeling that something wasn't right with Isaac.

Chapter Seven

The next morning, I was watching crappy morning TV when Lucy sat down next to me. "Hey, did you have a good night?"

"Don't ask" she replied.

"So that's a no then, are you okay?"

"I haven't decided."

"What has he done now?"

She blushed, "Who?"

"Dan, was he being a douche last night?"

"When is he *not* being a douche?"

"True. So what did he do to upset you?"

"I don't even want to waste my breath on him."

"Do you need me to kick him in the balls for you?"

"I already did."

I laughed, "Good. What did you end up doing in the end? You were out pretty late."

"Um, we just had a few drinks and then I stayed to watch some band play." She stood up, "Do you want a coffee?"

"No thanks, I'm leaving for class in a minute."

"More for me then."

***

I was on my way to class, making a mental note to kick Dan in the balls when Isaac called.

The wanderer returns.

"Hello" I answered.

"Hi, gorgeous."

"So, you're alive then."

He laughed, "Wait, let me check...yep, I have a pulse."

"Excellent" I replied, sarcastically.

"What's wrong?"

"Nothing."

"Okay, you're doing the dartboard thing again."

"What dartboard thing?"

"When you pretend that you're okay but you're not. You really want to put my face on a dartboard and aim for my eyes."

"Maybe you're the one who's pretending to be okay."

"And now you're using reverse psychology."

"Why would I use that?"

"Why *wouldn't* you use it?"

"Okay smartass, why didn't you call me last night?"

"I was really busy then I fell asleep, I'm sorry."

"Busy doing what?"

"I've got a lot of things to take care of these next few weeks. Anyway, enough about that. What did you get up to last night?"

I paused, debating the best way to tell him about my trip to see Lukas.

"Are you just going to ignore me?" he asked.

"No. Can I see you tonight? I'll tell you then." I wanted to speak to him about it face to face rather than over the phone. Then I could also ask him why he was acting so weird yesterday.

"Of course."

"Are you sure you're not too busy?" I asked with a little too much sass.

"Nope, I'm all yours."

***

I arrived at my lecture ten minutes early so decided to catch up on some reading from last week. I only managed to read two pages before Hollie came rushing over to me. She had a huge grin on her face and I could feel the excitement dripping off her. "April, you need to get your ass outside now."

"Good morning to you too" I replied.

She sighed, "Good morning April, you need to get your ass outside now."

"Why?"

"There's an insanely hot guy that you need to see."

I raised one eyebrow, "Last time you said that, it was Dan."

She laughed, "Dan's a solid eight out of ten but this guy's off the scale."

"Well thanks for the update but the lecture's going to start soon."

"Get your priorities straight, woman."

"Ohhhh, you're right. Who comes to University to actually study?"

"I'm always right, remember?" She winked at me but I had a feeling that there was some kind of hidden meaning behind it. "Fine, don't go. He asked for you but if you don't care then it's not a big deal."

"What do you mean he asked for me?"

Hollie laughed, "Woops, did I forget to mention that?"

"What did he say?"

"He asked if I knew you. I told him to wait outside while I checked if you were in here. I didn't want to blow your cover in case he's an ex or something."

"Or a stalker?"

"He's gorgeous, who cares if he's a stalker? He can stalk me any day."

"Who the hell is he?"

She giggled, "I didn't ask for his name, just his number."

I sighed, "What does he look like?"

"Hot." I waved, indicating for her to carry on. "Around six foot three, black hair, green eyes. Wanna know the best part? He's covered in tats, full sleeves."

"How old is he?"

She shrugged, "A few years older than us, maybe."

I stood up, having a sneaky suspicion of who it might be.

"Woop woop" Hollie yelled, "I knew you were a sucker for tats."

I shook my head at her before walking outside. I looked around but didn't see anybody matching her description. However, I did see a group of girls standing in a circle. It looked like they were gathered around something...or someone. As I got closer, I heard the sound of a motorbike mixed with lots of giggling. They looked like the Barbie Dolls who had been fawning over Isaac the night of the mixer. It wouldn't surprise me if it was the same group. I heard the engine cut off so took a step closer. The group of girls separated so I had a clear view. I cleared my throat, "Well, well, well, look who it is."

"Excuse me, Ladies." He got off his bike before walking over to me. He picked me up, hugging me tightly, "Hey, Sis."

I laughed, "What are you doing here?"

"I had to come and check that my little sister's okay." He took a step back, "You look different, have you been eating properly?"

"Shut up, it's only been six weeks."

"Well it seems like an eternity, I miss your face. I wanted to visit sooner but..." He stopped talking mid sentence.

"But what?"

He shrugged, "But I've been busy with work and the band and I knew you'd be busy too."

I watched the Barbie Dolls walk away and nodded in their direction, "I see you've made some friends already."

He grinned, "I like it here."

"Hmmm, I bet you do. How did you even know where to look for me?"

"The hot receptionist from the Student Union told me."

"Um, isn't that like a security breach or something?"

"I made up a story, she loved it."

"Enlighten me..."

"I told her that I flew all the way from Australia to surprise my little sister on her birthday. I said that we haven't seen each other for years, I put on an accent and everything. I found out what building you were in within minutes."

"That's actually pretty scary, I should probably report her."

"Don't worry, she only told me because of my good looks...and charm...and kick ass Australian accent. Oh, and I slipped her my number too."

"You've been here for what, less than an hour? And you're already on the lookout."

"It's a full time job."

I laughed, "How long are you staying for?"

He shrugged, "A couple of days, maybe a week. I'll see how it goes, I've not brought much with me."

I eyed his motorbike and the single backpack next to it. "Where are you planning on staying?"

"I'll find a hotel later. What time do you finish today?"

"Around four, I have classes all day. I'm staying with a friend, why don't you wait for me there? I'm sure she won't mind, I'll call her and check."

"Is she hot?"

I rolled my eyes as I pulled my phone out of my pocket. Lucy didn't pick up so I sent her a quick text -

"Hey. My Brother's here, he surprised me! I've said that he can hang out at the flat today until I finish my classes. Hope that's ok? He's harmless. See you later x"

I went back and deleted the part about him being harmless before sending it. I took out Lucy's spare key, "Go and ask your little receptionist friend to give you directions to number 17 Yew Tree Road, Flat 1A. It won't take long on that death trap of yours."

"Are you ever going to stop calling it that?"

"Are you ever going to stop riding it?"

"No chance."

"There's your answer. I'd better go, I'll see you around fourish." I gave him another hug before walking back to class. I looked over my shoulder, "Brody?"

"Yeah?"

"Be good."

He winked as he climbed onto his bike, "I'm always good."

Chapter Eight

I had a smile on my face for the rest of the day and was looking forward to spending some quality time with Brody. I called him twice in the day - once to check that he got to Lucy's okay and the other to check that he hadn't trashed the place.

As soon as my last class finished, I rushed back to the flat, texting Isaac on the way -

"Sorry, change of plan! My brother has come to visit so I'm going to spend some time with him tonight. See you tomorrow? xxx"

As soon as I walked through the door, Lucy ushered me back outside. "Is everything okay?" I asked.

"Is your brother adopted?"

I laughed, "Not to my knowledge, why?"

"He's the complete opposite of you."

"Well yeah, he's a man and I'm a woman."

"You know what I mean. He's so cocky."

"Has he been giving you a hard time?"

She blushed, "Nothing that I can't handle."

"I'm sorry, I shouldn't have sent him here without speaking to you first. I tried calling you but I didn't know what else to do, I had classes all day."

"No, it's fine. I would have done the same."

"If it makes you feel any better, he's like this with everybody."

"Yeah, he's been on the phone with two different girls already. I've been trying to guess which one is his girlfriend."

I laughed, "Brody doesn't do girlfriends."

"Well it sounded like he knew them pretty well, if you know what I mean."

I knew exactly what she meant. "No, how do you mean?"

"Well he was being rather...explicit."

"That's Brody for you."

"How long is he visiting for?" she asked.

"I don't know, I've not had the chance to speak to him properly yet."

"Just make it clear that he's to stay on the sofa."

"Oh, you don't have to offer him a place to stay. He can check into a hotel later."

"He's your brother, of course he can stay here."

"Are you sure?"

"Yeah, now let's go back inside before I change my mind."

I hugged her, "Thank you, it should only be for a few days."

Brody stood up when we walked back inside. "Ladies, can you make it less obvious when you talk about me next time?"

I picked up a cushion and threw it at his head, "The world doesn't revolve around you."

He caught Lucy's arm as she walked by, "Look me in the eye and tell me that you weren't talking about me."

She looked down at his hand, "I might only be five foot three but I can still kick your ass."

He grinned as he let go of her arm, "Is that a promise? I like it rough."

Lucy scowled at him before disappearing into her bedroom.

"So, where am I taking you for dinner?" he asked me.

"I know an awesome Italian place."

***

Brody seemed impressed by the restaurant and pretty much ordered one of everything. While Brody was impressed by the food, I was impressed by the fact that he didn't flirt with the waitress. Trust me, it was a rare occurrence.

After placing our orders, we sipped our chocolate milkshakes and it brought back memories of when we were kids, "I'm glad you're here."

His grin matched mine, "Me too, I miss your nagging."

I gasped, "I do not nag."

"Let's agree to disagree."

"I disagree with your agreement to disagree."

"Well I disagree with your disagreement to agree to disagree."

I cocked my head to one side, "Well I disagree with your disagreement of my...oh hell."

He whooped, "I always win."

I scowled as I took another sip of my milkshake, "Catch me up on what's been happening back home. How have you been?"

"This isn't a counselling session, I don't care if you're studying it."

"I know it's not" I replied, defensively. "This is a sister asking her brother how he's been."

He narrowed his eyes, "Is that what they teach you to say?"

I rolled mine, "Shut up."

"Respect your elders."

"Respect...women."

"I always do."

I raised my eyebrow, "Is that right?"

"Yep, I respect their *needs*."

I burst out laughing, "Too much information. So come on, what's been happening back home?"

"I almost forgot how much of a mind ninja you were."

I snorted, "Mind ninja?"

He tapped his temple, "Yeah, you're like a ninja trying to get inside my head. I'm fine, life's fine, everything's fine."

"Oh yeah? Is Mum fine?"

He sighed, "Let's not do this now. Can't you just be happy that I'm here?"

I knew that he was trying to avoid talking about her. "Of course I'm happy that you're here but I need to know how she is. Is she sober?"

My mother made a promise to me the night before I left for University. She looked me in the eye and promised me that she would be completely sober by the time I came home for Christmas break. My heartbeat sped up as I waited for Brody to answer but he didn't need to. His face said it all.

"She's in rehab."

I laughed because I knew that if I didn't, I would cry. "What happened this time?"

He shrugged, "Same old. She drank too much, I called an ambulance, she went to rehab. End of story."

The whole situation was messed up. A son and daughter shouldn't have to talk this way about their own mother. Especially talking about it like it was the most normal thing in the world. I shook my head, "When did she check in?"

"Yesterday." He placed his head in his hands, "Is it wrong that I'm actually a little bit relieved? Relieved that I don't have to look after her? Don't have to worry about her choking on her own sick? Is it wrong that I'm glad to finally have some time to visit my little sister?"

I shook my head as I fought back the tears. "No, it's not wrong."

The waitress chose that exact moment to bring over our food. We ate in comfortable silence for a few minutes before Brody spoke, "So..."

"So?" I asked.

I knew what was about to happen. I bit my lip to stop myself from laughing. Every now and again, Brody liked to play the overprotective big brother.

"Are you dating?"

Yes, I'm in a serious relationship with my personal tutor.

"Nope" I lied.

"Why not?"

I rolled my eyes at his stupid question, "Because I'm a strong independent woman." He looked at me with his eyebrow raised, waiting for me to carry on. I sighed dramatically, "Maybe I'm not pretty enough."

"Bullshit, there's not a single guy in here who hasn't checked you out. Which, by the way, is starting to piss me off." I blushed as I looked around the restaurant, suddenly feeling self conscious. "Are you telling me the truth? You're really not dating?"

"I'm really not dating."

Technically, it was the truth. I wasn't dating. If he were to ask me if I was in a secret relationship with my tutor, then that would be a completely different story.

He took a long drink of his milkshake, keeping his eyes on mine the whole time. "Good. If you do decide to date, you should wait until you're married before you do anything."

I burst out laughing, "I will if you will."

"Well that wouldn't be fair."

"And why is that?"

"Because I'm never getting married."

"That's what they all say until they meet the game changer."

"I don't want somebody changing my game, I'm too busy."

I sighed, "So many girls, so little time."

"Speaking of which, when are you going to introduce me to your hot friends?"

"How about never?" I replied.

"How about tomorrow?" I folded my arms across my chest. "Aww don't be like that, Sis."

"Well you've already met Hollie."

"Is she single?"

"Um, I don't actually know. She's kind of seeing someone."

"Well it doesn't matter anyway." He winked at me, earning him a slap on the wrist.

"What about Lucy? What's her deal?"

"She's single and way too nice for most of the jerks around here."

"Good job I'm not from around here then."

"What about the jerk part?"

He laughed, "I'm not *most* jerks."

"You know the rules, stay away from my friends. There's plenty of girls on campus, go and break their hearts instead."

He feigned innocence, "I don't know what you're talking about."

"Sure you don't. Lucy said you can crash on the sofa while you're here."

"And by the sofa she means..."

"The sofa. What else could that mean?"

He raised his eyebrow, "You'd be surprised."

"She's doing us both a big favour by letting us stay with her so you need to be on your best behaviour." He grinned before saluting me. "So how's work?" I asked, before taking another bite of pizza.

"It pays the bills."

"Have you seen much of Katie and Ian?"

"Yeah, I saw her walking Jamie when I was out running last week. She said that she misses you. I'll go round and check on her soon, make sure Ian's treating her right."

I grinned, "You're the best."

"Oh, before I forget, I've brought you a CD with some new tracks on. I want your opinion."

I grinned, "Speaking of which, how is the band?"

His eyes lit up, "Awesome, we've been recording a lot of new stuff recently. We've sent it off to a few big shots."

I loved listening to him talk about his band. *'We Say Summer'* formed when he was fifteen, just after my mum started drinking heavily. It started out as an escape for him but now it was his entire life. He lived for his music, even his body was covered in song lyrics and musical notes.

"Well let's hope that these big shots can recognise good music when they hear it."

He held his milkshake up, "Cheers to that."

***

Lucy was already in bed by the time we got back. I noticed a pile of blankets on the sofa as I made my way to the kitchen. "Do you want a glass of water?"

"No thanks, I'll be back in a minute." I watched as he walked over to Lucy's bedroom door.

"Woah, where are you going?"

"I want to say thanks to Lucy."

I frowned, "It's late and she's probably asleep, can't you thank her tomorrow?"

"It's nine thirty."

"And?" I asked.

"Nobody goes to bed at nine thirty, not even good girls."

"How would you know? You don't exactly surround yourself with good girls."

He gave me his best cocky grin, "They all start off good."

"Hang on...are you saying that *you* turn them bad?"

"Your words, not mine."

I snorted, "Oh wow, I almost forgot how big headed you were."

Lucy's door swung open, "Everything okay?"

"Perfect" Brody replied after a short pause.

Lucy took a step back and crossed her arms over her chest.

"Sorry if we woke you" I told her.

"You didn't, I was reading."

"What were you reading?" Brody asked.

"A book, you should try it some time."

"Ouch! I read."

"Girls phone numbers don't count" she added. I couldn't help but laugh.

Brody smirked, "How stereotypical of you."

"Okay then, what's the last thing that you read?"

He pulled a piece of paper out of his back pocket and began to read, "Call me. 07750..." Lucy tried to close the door but he held his arm out.

"What do you want?" she asked.

I didn't hear his response but whatever he said made her blush and then slam the door in his face. He walked over to me, laughing.

"I thought you just wanted to say thanks?"

"I did, you mustn't have heard."

"No, but I heard the door slam. I meant what I said before."

"What, that I'm the best? Again, your words not mine."

"You better be on your best behaviour around here, you've been warned."

He winked, "Then you better warn Lucy too."

Chapter Nine

The next morning, I woke up to an empty flat. Lucy had early classes on a Wednesday and Brody was nowhere to be seen. I had some breakfast before heading out to class.

My day was mediocre up until lunch time when I decided to pay Isaac a little visit. I smiled as I remembered his phone call last night. After we got back from the Italian, he called to ask how Brody was and to tell me how much he missed me. He sounded tired but was back to his usual self. I put his weirdness the other day down to him being busy with work.

As I walked down the corridor, I began to question what I was doing but the excitement of what could happen next kept me going. I waited outside his door for a few seconds. When I couldn't hear any voices inside, I knocked.

"Come in" he shouted. He smiled and took off his glasses when he saw me, "Hey you, is everything okay?"

I closed the door behind me before locking it, "It is now." I took a deep breath before slowly taking off my coat, followed by my jumper. I began to unbutton my jeans when he stood up, "Stop."

Oh no, I'd made a huge mistake by coming here. It was far too risky to try anything in his office. I went to pick up my jumper as he walked towards me, "Stop, I should be undressing you."

My heart began to pound out of my chest as he picked me up and carried me over to his desk. He lay me down and pulled my jeans off in one swift movement. Within seconds, his mouth was all over my body, kissing every inch of skin. He started on my neck before working his way down. By the time he reached my thighs, I felt like I was going to explode.

I glanced at the door, unsure whether I was going to be able to stay quiet. What if somebody heard us? "Are you sure about this?"

"I've never been so sure of anything in my life."

"Are you expecting anybody to come here?"

He grinned, "You." He pinned my arms above my head before slowly taking off my knickers, "Do you know how many times I've fantasised about this?"

"About the same amount of times that I have?"

"More. Way more." I gasped when I felt his mouth right where I needed him the most. He started off slow before gradually picking up the pace. "You taste so fucking good." He used his fingers to create the perfect combination. As if what he was actually doing to me wasn't enough, I had the absolute pleasure of watching him do it. I couldn't take my eyes off him, it was completely mesmerising. It took all of my strength not to scream out his name. "Do you like that, baby?"

"Yes, yes, yes" I replied, incapable of saying anything else.

"Not as much as I like doing it." His tongue moved even faster and I could feel myself climbing. He moaned against me and that was all it took. My eyes rolled to the back of my head as pleasure washed over me. He carried on until he was sure that I had nothing left to give. "Apologies in advance."

"What for?" I whispered.

"I'm the horniest man alive, this isn't going to last very long."

I heard the sound of his zipper before he pushed into me. I wrapped my legs around his waist and pulled him closer, urging him in deeper. He withdrew completely before thrusting back in. He was still wearing his shirt and tie and the reality of what we were doing hit me. It was so sexy, I could feel the pressure starting to build once more. His eyes were fiery and intense as he pulled me off the table and flipped me over. My palms found his desk as he slammed into me from behind. "Isaac..."

"Come with me, baby."

His order was enough to tip me over the edge. My body went completely limp as I swam in a sea of pleasure, letting the waves take me under. Isaac growled before collapsing on top of me.

"I can't remember if I even said hello."

He grinned as he helped me up off his desk, "You didn't. Hello."

I laughed, "Hello. You've been holding out on me, Mr Sharpe."

"How so?"

"You've made me wait all this time to experience *that*."

"Well I needed to make sure that you weren't just using me for *that*."

"I have a feeling that you'll be using it a lot more from now on."

He laughed, "My pleasure."

I shook my head, "Trust me, the pleasure will be all mine."

He kissed me before picking my clothes up off the floor. "There's no chance in hell that I'm going to get any work done this afternoon. How am I supposed to concentrate now?"

"Sorry" I replied, sweetly.

He grinned, "No need to apologise, that should keep me going until the next time I see you. Speaking of which, do you know when that will be?"

"I don't know, whenever Brody gets bored of me."

"I wish that I could meet him."

"Me too."

"You should bring him into the bar one night."

"Hmmm, I'm not sure..."

"Why not?"

"I've not told him about us yet, I don't know how he'd react. I'd rather wait until you finish working here."

"We don't have to tell him, you could introduce me as your friend. I'll ply him with alcohol so he doesn't suspect anything."

"Hmmm, are you sure you're going to be able to keep your hands off me?"

"I can't promise anything."

I laughed, "I'll think about it."

After nearly ending up on his desk for a second time, I left his office with rosy cheeks and a huge smile.

Chapter Ten

My good mood carried on for the rest of the day and I practically skipped home from class. When I got back to Lucy's, I was greeted by the smell of something cooking.

"Hey, Sis" Brody shouted from the kitchen.

I went to investigate. "Hey, what's cooking?"

"Chicken curry."

We high fived. "God, I've missed your curries. What's it in aid of?"

"I wanted to cook for my little sister and say thank you to Lucy for letting me crash."

I leaned up on my tiptoes to ruffle his hair, "See, you can be sweet. So how's your day been?"

"Interesting, yours?"

"Interesting." I blushed as I thought back to my earlier antics. "You were up early this morning."

"Yeah, I gave Lucy a ride to class."

I raised my eyebrow in question.

"She was running late."

"Well that's nice of you."

"Try telling her that, I had to force her onto my bike. She wanted to walk even though she was already ten minutes late."

I heard the front door open before Lucy joined us in the kitchen a few seconds later. She eyed Brody suspiciously.

"Speak of the devil" I said.

She laughed, "What have I done now?"

"You tell me. How was your day?"

"Good, thanks."

"She had her legs spread and her body pressed up against mine, of course it was good. You don't have to downplay it, you can admit how awesome it was."

"That won't be happening ever again."

He laughed, "That's what you think."

"In your dreams."

"Actually, we don't wear any clothes in my dreams. Do you want me to show you?"

She blushed, "You're crazy."

"I'd rather be crazy than in denial."

I sighed before taking a seat at the kitchen table, "Play nice, children."

Lucy took a seat next to me, "Did your brother tell you what happened this morning?"

"Yep, he gave you a ride to class because you were late."

"Oh no, he *kidnapped* me and then drove the long way to class."

Brody winked at me, "I'm new around here, I didn't know that there was a shorter route."

She gasped, "We actually drove past the University. *Twice.* You know, that huge building with the University logo on it?"

"I was concentrating on the road."

"Didn't you wonder why I was squeezing you so damn hard?"

"No, I just thought you wanted to grope me."

She rolled her eyes, "Well thanks for making me even later, it would have been faster for me to walk."

"But a lot less fun." He walked over to the table with two plates of curry, "Please accept this as my apology."

She sighed, "This actually looks pretty good."

"Don't sound so surprised" Brody replied as he walked back into the kitchen for his plate.

I laughed before digging in.

***

"So what are we doing tonight?" Brody asked after we finished eating.

"Well, the last time I checked, we were sitting at the kitchen table" I replied.

He grinned, "Wow, you definitely got the funny gene. Let's go out for a drink, I'm paying."

"I can't" Lucy answered.

"You busy reading? Have you got one of those candle things?"

"It's a *kindle* and no, I'm actually going to a friend's house."

"And by friend you mean boyfriend?"

She frowned, "No, I mean friend." She looked at me, "A few of us are going to see Lukas, he's feeling a lot better. I think he's getting fed up of staying in the house on his own."

"See, it is a man."

We both ignored him. "Do you want to come?" she asked me.

"We'll go" Brody replied before I even had the chance to say anything.

"Woah, woah, woah..."

"What? Do you not know this Lukas guy?"

Um, long story.

"I know him."

"Then let's go. You heard what Lucy said, the poor guy's getting bored." He turned to face Lucy, "Wait, why is he getting bored?"

Lucy looked at me before standing up, "I'm going to get changed. Thanks for dinner, Brody."

He winked, "You can thank me later."

I waited until I heard Lucy's bedroom door close before speaking, "I don't think it's a good idea."

"Why not?"

"Me and Lukas...we have a history."

The muscles in his jaw tensed, "What happened?"

"We're better off as friends."

"Who ended it?"

"Me."

"Did he hurt you?"

Yes but I also hurt him.

"No."

"You had to think about that one."

"It wasn't meant to be, we've moved on."

"What did Lucy mean when she said that he's doing better? Has that got something to do with you?"

I paused for a moment, trying to find the right words. "The fire at my house...he was trapped inside."

Brody's eyes widened, "He's the guy?" I nodded. "No wonder his name sounded familiar. Okay, we're definitely going, I need to shake his hand."

A thousand things were running through my mind but there was one thought that stood out the most. My brother was about to meet Lukas before meeting Isaac. It might not be a big deal to other people but it was to me. It just didn't seem right.

I sighed, "Okay but I want to go somewhere else first."

Chapter Eleven

An hour later, all three of us walked into Sienna's.

"What are we doing here?" Lucy whispered.

"I wanted a drink before we go to see Lukas" I lied.

She nodded, "I understand."

I couldn't see Isaac anywhere. I called him a few times before we set off but he didn't answer. He probably wasn't even here, making this a wasted trip.

"What can I get for you?" The bartender asked Brody.

"I'll have a beer. Ladies?"

"Red wine please" I replied, keeping an eye out for Isaac.

"Lucy?"

"I'm good, thanks."

"That's good to know but what do you want to drink?"

"Nothing, I'm good."

Brody turned to the bartender, "Two red wines, please."

"I hope you didn't just order me a drink."

"Red wine isn't really my thing and I'm not about to get my sister wasted so..."

"I won't drink it."

"What kind of student are you?" he asked.

"One that actually studies."

I tuned them both out when I saw Isaac walk out from the back room, followed closely by Abbie. She had a huge grin on her face as she whispered something to him. He ran a hand through his hair before turning away from her. He froze when his eyes locked onto mine. Abbie's grin turned even bigger.

Lucy nudged me, "Earth to April."

I shook my head, "Sorry, what?"

"I asked if you knew that Mr Sharpe worked here?"

"Um yeah, he mentioned it in one of our meetings. I don't think they get paid much for being a personal tutor."

"He's so hot."

"Oh please, he's just a pretty boy" Brody replied.

"That's my point."

My heart felt like it was going to hammer its way out of my chest. The look on Abbie's face had completely thrown me for a loop. "I'll be back in a minute, I'm just going to the Ladies room."

Brody nodded, "I'll get a table, Lucy can help me carry the drinks."

I hurried off in the direction of the toilets and then hovered outside. When Isaac appeared a few seconds later, I was shocked when he pulled me into the Men's toilets.

"Are you serious? What's up with the stockroom?" I asked.

"Shhhhh." He pulled me into a toilet cubicle before locking the door. "What is wrong with you? Why were you looking at me like that just then?"

"Like what?"

"You're obviously upset, is it because Abbie's here?"

"I tried calling you. Three times."

"Sorry, I left my phone upstairs."

"What were you doing in the back with her?"

He glowered at me, "Working."

"What did she whisper to you?"

"April, what the fuck are you doing?"

I frowned, confused as to why he was getting angry. "Um, right now I'm in a toilet cubicle with my secret boyfriend..."

He held his hand over my mouth. The reason soon became clear when I heard footsteps. We literally stared at each other for a whole minute straight until the person left and Isaac was satisfied that we were completely alone. He removed his hand from my mouth, "Don't taint what we have."

"Me?" I asked, shocked.

"Do you trust me?"

"Yes."

"Then don't ask me ridiculous questions ever again."

"Fuck you."

He raised his eyebrows, "Fuck me?"

"Yes, fuck you. I wouldn't ask ridiculous questions if I didn't have a reason to. Answer your fucking phone next time, employ a fucking sane person to be the manager of your bar next time, tell people to stop whispering in your fucking ear next time."

I tried to unlock the door but he held his arm out, "April, I'm sorry for snapping at you. I've had a stressful night and then I walked into the bar and saw your beautiful face. It should have cheered me up but the first thing I saw was the doubt in your eyes."

"Yeah and the first thing I saw was Abbie whispering in your ear."

"You know what she's like..."

"Oh, so that makes it okay then?"

"I didn't mean it like that. It's best to keep her on our side for now, just until I finish working at the University. I've told you how manipulative she can be."

"And by manipulative you mean a bitch?"

"Well, yeah." He let go of the door, "Look, I don't want you to doubt me, to doubt us. That's the kind of shit that destroys a relationship. Doubt takes something good and taints it, I won't let that happen. You're the only one for me and the whole world will know it soon enough."

I sighed, "You're right, I'm sorry. You know my feelings towards her but I shouldn't take it out on you."

"Let me handle Abbie, you've got nothing to worry about. Okay?" I nodded. "It'll all be over soon." He kissed my forehead, "Seven days."

"And counting. I'd better go before Brody comes looking for me."

"Thanks for bringing him here, I'm happy that I get to meet him."

I nodded, "I wanted you to meet him first."

"First?"

"We're going to see Lukas."

He raised his eyebrows, "Oh."

"Lucy invited us, I didn't want to go but Brody said that he wanted to."

"It's okay, he's your friend. You can make your own decisions, I'll always respect them." I could see in his eyes that he truly meant it. He laughed, "Now go, before I get beaten up by your brother, he's bigger than I expected."

Isaac made sure that the coast was clear before I left the toilets and walked back into the bar. I rolled my eyes when I saw Abbie sitting next to Brody, giggling at something that he was saying.

So much for the overprotective big brother coming to rescue me.

"Oh, hi April" she said, when she noticed me. I nodded in response as I sat down next to Lucy. "Why didn't you tell me that your brother was so handsome?"

"Are you nearly ready to go?" Lucy asked before downing a glass of red wine.

Brody smirked, "I thought you weren't going to drink it?"

"I changed my mind."

I took a big gulp of my own.

"I heard about the fire, I can't believe that someone would do such a thing. How are you coping?" Abbie asked.

"I'm fine."

"How's your friend? The one who was trapped?"

"Lukas. He's getting better."

"That's good to hear."

I looked over her shoulder to see Isaac approaching. "Hey, sorry to interrupt. Abbie, can you cover the bar? Charlie's taking his break now."

Abbie continued to look at me for a few more seconds before standing up, "Of course." She placed her hand on Brody's shoulder, "See you around." He watched as she strutted over to the bar.

Isaac extended his hand to Brody, "Hey, I'm Isaac."

They shook hands. "Brody."

"Isaac's my tutor" I told him.

"Why do you work here if you have a job at the University?"

"I actually own this place."

"So then I guess the question should be, why do you work at the University if you own this place?"

Isaac laughed, "I finish working there next week."

Brody looked around, "You've got a nice place."

"Thanks." He gestured towards the piano, "Do you play?"

"I play guitar in a band."

"He's incredible" I added.

"You've got to say that, you're my sister."

"Your *honest* sister."

Isaac laughed, "What's your band called?"

"We Say Summer."

"No way, I went to one of your gigs a few years ago at the Roadhouse. My little sister loved you."

Brody's eyes lit up, "That's awesome, small world."

"It is. Look, if you're ever in the area, the stage is all yours."

"Cheers, man."

"Well I better get back to work, it was good to meet you. You should come back some time, drinks are on the house."

"In that case, I'll be here every night."

Isaac laughed before turning to face me. He smiled reassuringly, "Have a great evening."

I nodded, "You too." I tried my best not to watch him as he walked away.

We finished our drinks and then made our way out of the bar. After a few minutes, Brody turned to face me, "He seems nice."

I felt like jumping up and down. Instead, I shrugged, trying my best to play it cool.

Chapter Twelve

"You didn't tell me that it was a party" I said as we stepped into Lukas's flat.

"I didn't *know* that it was a party." Lucy replied, "I bet Dan had something to do with it."

"Who's Dan?" Brody asked.

"Dan the dickhead" Lucy muttered.

I laughed, "What she said."

"Want me to have a quiet word with him?" he asked.

Now it was Lucy's turn to laugh, "Sounds good to me. April?"

"Stop trying to get my brother into trouble."

"I like trouble" Brody replied as we made our way into the kitchen to get some drinks. I recognised a few people from my classes but couldn't see Lukas anywhere. I groaned when I spotted Dan walking towards us.

He slapped Lucy on the ass, making her cheeks turn fire red. "Woop woop, my bitches have arrived!"

I saw anger flash across Brody's eyes as he took a step forward, "You must be Dan."

"Who's asking?"

"Well let's just say that I don't take nicely to people calling my sister a bitch."

"Chill out, I was only joking."

"I don't care what you were doing, you still don't get to call her a bitch. Or Lucy for that matter."

"What's your problem?"

"You are."

"Well that's funny because you're in *my* flat, so why don't you just go ahead and leave?"

Lukas suddenly appeared at our side, "It's also *my* flat and I want him to stay, stop being a dick to our guests."

"Whose side are you on?" Dan asked.

"Isn't that obvious?"

"Fuck this" Dan announced as he turned to face me and Lucy, "You know I was only joking, he needs to chill out."

"And you need to learn to show some respect" Brody replied.

Dan took a step backwards before gesturing to some other guys, "Come on, let's get out of here."

I watched them leave, thankful that Brody wasn't about to get into a fight.

"I thought he said a quiet word?" Lucy whispered.

"Trust me, that was quiet for him."

"Closet alpha" she muttered.

"There's no closet about it" I replied.

Brody turned to Lukas, "Are his parents cops? Or lawyers?"

Lukas laughed, "Nah, I think they own a cake shop."

He winked at me, "Just checking, I like to know what I'm getting myself into beforehand."

"No, stop it now. No more arguments, no fighting. I mean it, we're guests here."

He held his hands up in surrender, "Okay, okay."

Lukas extended his hand, "I'm Lukas, nice to meet you."

Brody cocked his head to the side, "*The* Lukas?" I rolled my eyes at how dramatic he was.

Lukas laughed, "It depends what you've heard."

"I've heard how you tried to save my sister's life. Seriously, I can't thank you enough."

"I'd do it again in a heartbeat."

"Good man, that's what I like to hear. I feel better knowing that there are people looking out for her when I'm not around."

"I'll always be here for her, she knows that."

I smiled as we made our way over to the sofa.

Brody and Lukas got on like a house on fire.

Excuse the pun.

After twenty minutes of football talk, I stood up, "I'm going to get some fresh air."

"Want me to come with you?" Lucy asked.

"No, stay here, make sure Brody behaves." I needed a few minutes on my own. Last week, Lukas was lying in a hospital bed fighting for his life and now he was talking football with my brother. The whole situation was a little overwhelming. Everything had moved so fast since the fire and I needed time to get my head around it all.

I sat on the brick wall outside and looked up at the stars. It always reminded me that there were much bigger things going on in the world. I was still gazing up at the sky when Brody sat next to me. "You okay?" he asked, draping his arm around my shoulders.

"Yeah, I just needed some air."

"Are you mad at me for what happened with Dan?"

"No, I just don't want you causing any trouble."

"I won't." We were silent for a little while before he turned to face me, "Lukas is a nice guy."

"He is."

"I can see how much he cares for you." I nodded. "But you're in love with someone else..."

"What?"

"I can read you like a book, how long have you been in love with your tutor?"

I looked around us, paranoid in case anybody was eavesdropping on our conversation. Brody stood up, "Walk with me." We began to walk down the street. "So? What's happening with you and Isaac?"

I took a deep breath, "I will never speak to you again if you lay a finger on him, I mean it."

"Calm down, what do you take me for? I like Isaac."

"You do?"

"Yeah, he's a nice guy. It's obvious that he has feelings for you too."

And there was me thinking that we were doing a good job of hiding our feelings.

Brody smirked, "Don't disappear together for as long next time." I blushed. "So come on, what's happening?"

"I met him on my first day before any of us knew that he was my tutor. The attraction was instant and we arranged to meet up the day after."

"So what happened when you found out that he was your tutor?"

"Nothing happened. Well, Lukas happened. We grew close and..." I shook my head, "Things happened when they shouldn't have. It was always meant to be Isaac. I tried to fight it but I couldn't turn my feelings off."

"Does Lukas know about him?"

"Yes, he found out the day before the fire."

"And he's agreed not to say anything?" I nodded. "Then he's a good friend."

"I know. We've both made mistakes but I want us to move on."

"So is that why Isaac's quitting his job at the University? So you two can be together?"

"Yeah, it was his decision."

"Are you ready for the backlash?"

"After everything that's happened, I don't care about the backlash. I just want to be with him."

"And you're one hundred percent sure that he's the one?"

"One hundred percent, without a shadow of a doubt."

"Then I'll support you. Just make sure that he treats you right and if he doesn't, let me know."

I laughed, "I won't need to but thanks."

"Does Lucy know?"

"No, only Lukas and Katie."

"Katie knows? She's got one hell of a poker face. I was grilling her last week to find out if you were dating and she didn't say a word."

"That's what best friends are for."

***

When we got back to Lucy's a couple of hours later, I felt like a giant weight had been lifted off my shoulders. Brody took the news about me and Isaac surprisingly well. Not only that but he actually admitted to liking Isaac which was a pretty big deal considering he usually hated it when a man even looked at me. Tonight had also proved that Lukas and I could still be friends. I wanted things to go back to the way they were before everything got complicated.

Brody yawned as he walked over to Lucy, "I'm tired, are you coming to bed?"

"*I'm* going to bed, you're on the sofa" she replied.

He crouched down, "You're sitting on the sofa right now so technically, you're in my bed. Do you want to go on top or bottom? I'm a fan of both."

Her face turned beetroot red, "You're such a pig."

"I've been called worse."

"Brody, leave her alone" I told him.

He whispered something to her before standing up and walking into the bathroom. A few seconds later, I heard the shower running.

"Just ignore him" I told her.

"Trust me, I'm trying. The problem is, he's pretty hard to ignore."

Chapter Thirteen

The next morning, I decided to call Isaac before getting ready for class.

"Hey beautiful, I was just thinking about you."

"Hey smooth talker, I hope they were good thoughts" I replied.

"Of course."

"Maybe you could tell me all about them tonight, how does six thirty sound?"

"It sounds awesome. Are you sure you don't mind leaving Brody?"

"I'll ask Lucy to keep him entertained."

"I'm glad that I got to meet him last night."

"He knows about us" I blurted out.

"Oh, okay. Did you tell him?"

"No, apparently we're not very good actors. He asked me last night so I told him the truth."

"How did he take it?"

"He's fine, just don't break my heart or he will kick your ass."

"You know that I would never break your heart. Does that mean you can both come round tonight for a family meal?"

"Don't push your luck."

He laughed, "So how did last night go?"

"It went okay, I had a nice time."

"I'm glad. How's Lukas doing?"

"Better, he should be back in class soon."

"That's good, did you get the chance to talk to him?"

I pondered whether or not to tell him that I went to see him on Monday. But then I didn't want him to wonder why I hadn't told him straight away.

"April?"

"Um, yeah a little bit but Brody was doing most of the talking."

"Well I'm glad that he's doing okay. Look, I've got to go, I'll see you tonight."

I got dressed before going in search of coffee. Lucy was sat at the kitchen table reading a book. "Morning, do you want a coffee?"

She pointed to her orange juice, "No thanks."

"Where's Brody?"

She shrugged, "I haven't seen him."

"Could you do me a big favour?"

"Sure."

"Could you keep him entertained for a few hours tonight?"

She sighed, "Why?"

"I said that I'd meet one of my friends for a catch up."

"A boy?"

"You're getting as bad as him, it's just a friend."

She laughed, "I'm sure he can look after himself for a few hours."

"I know but I feel bad leaving him on his own when he's come here to spend time with me. Maybe you could go and watch a movie or something? It'll keep him out of trouble. Please?"

"Okay, no need for the puppy dog eyes."

I grinned, "Thank you."

"You're welcome. Oh and before I forget, some post came for you this morning." She handed me a letter and a parcel.

"Thank you, are you sure it's okay for me to give this address out until I get my own place?"

"Of course, I don't mind at all."

"You're the best."

I recognised Katie's handwriting on the parcel straight away. It was probably safer to open it when I was alone.

***

I was right.

I sat on my bed and pulled out her note -

"See, I wasn't joking. Hope you both like it xo"

I was confused by her cryptic message until I pulled out the contents. Thank god I didn't open it in front of Lucy after all.

It was a T-shirt.

A *Team Isaac* T-shirt.

I burst out laughing before trying it on. After opening the other letter, I called my crazy best friend.

"Guess what I'm wearing?" I asked as soon as she picked up.

"Oh la la, now I know why Isaac likes you so much."

"I'm wearing my new T-shirt."

"Oh, well that's boring. Does that usually get him going? Cos it's not doing much for me. What are you wearing underneath it?"

I laughed, "I'm wearing the T-shirt that you sent me."

She whooped, "I totally forgot about that, do you like it?"

"I love it. It's a good job I opened it when I was on my own."

"Oh shit, it's a good job Brody wasn't there."

"Brody knows about me and Isaac."

"What?!" she shouted, nearly deafening me.

"Brody knows, I told him last night."

"Are you crazy? Brody is *so* gonna kick Isaac's ass."

"No he won't, he was really supportive."

"Supportive of kicking Isaac's ass."

"Stop saying that."

"The truth hurts."

I laughed, "Shut up, he was fine about it. He likes Isaac."

"Has he met him?" she screeched.

"Yep, last night."

"I don't speak to you for a day and look what happens. I need details!"

"We went to the bar for a drink, I introduced Isaac as my tutor."

"So you didn't tell Brody until afterwards?"

"He asked me about an hour later when we were at Lukas's place, he suspected something."

"Um, rewind!" she shouted. "Why were you at Lukas's?"

"Stop shouting. Lucy invited us and Brody wanted to go."

"Okay, you're going to have to text me once an hour from now on. I can't keep up with your crazy life, you should have your own reality TV show."

"I sit in class every day, it's not that crazy. Speaking of which, I better head out."

She sighed, "Just when it was getting good."

I laughed, "Thanks for my T-shirt. I miss you."

"Miss you too. Let me know how Isaac is later after Brody kicks his ass."

"Bye Katie."

"I hope he doesn't break too many bones."

"Bye."

***

After my classes had finished, I walked into the flat and was greeted by the sound of an acoustic guitar. Brody smiled when he saw me but carried on playing. I sat down next to Lucy, "Oh, how I've missed that sound."

She turned to face me, "Hey, I didn't hear you come in."

"I'm stealthy like that. Where did he get the guitar from?"

"It was my Dads, it was collecting dust in my bedroom."

"That's nice of you. I hope you know that we won't be getting any sleep from now on, our neighbours back home always complain because he never shuts up."

"He never shut up *before* he got the guitar."

We both laughed, "True."

Brody stopped playing, "Charming. I'm going to make a start on dinner."

"What's with all the cooking, Gordon Ramsay?"

He raised his eyebrow, "Number one, I am miles younger and better looking than Gordon Ramsay. Number two, I'm not used to a student diet, I can't survive on noodles."

"Me caveman, me need protein" Lucy replied.

"I'll show you what I need later on."

She blushed as she watched him walk away. "Are you eating with us before you go out?"

"No, I'm getting in the shower then heading out. It's really sweet of you to let Brody use your Dads guitar."

She shrugged, "You asked me to keep him entertained."

"Well he won't bother you now that he's got his favourite toy."

"I thought his bike was his favourite toy?"

"Guitar then bike."

Brody walked back into the room, "Actually it's *women*, guitar and then bike."

***

Half an hour later, I was dressed to impressed. Lucy wolf whistled when I came out of my bedroom, "You look lovely, have fun with your *friend.*"

I pointed at Brody, "Have fun with yours." She rolled her eyes. "Try not to kill each other while I'm gone."

"I can't promise anything" she replied.

Brody walked me to the door before giving me a knowing look, "Stay safe, call me if you need me."

I groaned, "Okay Dad, don't wait up."

Chapter Fourteen

Isaac was sat by the back door waiting for me, "Hey beautiful."

"Hey yourself." I squealed when he picked me up and carried me inside. "Aren't I supposed to be wearing a long white dress when this happens?"

He grinned, "That can be arranged."

I gasped when we got inside his apartment. There were candles on every surface and soft music playing in the background. My heart melted when I realised that it was our song that was playing - *'I won't give up'* by *Jason Mraz*.

"Wow, it's beautiful." He placed me down before leading me over to the table, which was immaculately set. He pulled out a chair for me and poured us a glass of wine each. "What's all this for?"

He grinned, "You."

***

After wowing me with his cooking abilities, we moved over to the sofa. "Thank you, that was delicious."

"Are you ready for desert?"

I sat up, "Oooh, we're having desert?"

He raised his eyebrow and I immediately understood what that meant.

Communication by eyebrow.

"Ah ha, *that* kind of desert."

"If you mean the delicious kind then yes, I've heard it's your favourite."

"Well you've heard right."

He gave me a cocky grin, "I don't blame you...it's just so smooth and creamy."

Two can play that game.

"I love how it melts in my mouth" I replied, trying to keep a straight face.

"Oh really? I need a demonstration." He stood up and walked towards the kitchen. A few seconds later, he reappeared holding something behind his back.

"What are you hiding?"

"Your desert, of course."

I narrowed my eyes, "I'm starting to think that we've just been talking about two different things."

He shook his head and revealed the tub of chocolate body paint.

I laughed, "We are *so* not doing this."

"We *so* are."

"You're crazy" I told him.

"Crazy for you."

"Stop trying to sweet talk me."

He winked, "Good one, I see what you did there. Sweet talk...chocolate, now take off your clothes."

"But how will you know if I'm just using you for your chocolate?"

He slowly sauntered towards me, never once taking his eyes away from mine. My heart began to race as he bent down and whispered in my ear, "I'll take the risk if you take off your clothes."

"Deal" I replied before pulling my top up and over my head. I wriggled out of my jeans making sure that I never broke eye contact with him. It was pretty pathetic how turned on I could get just by looking at him. His intense glare ignited something deep inside of me. As the seconds ticked by, it was quite obvious that we were in some sort of competition, both refusing to be the one to look away first.

I hated losing.

I raised my eyebrow, challenging him, as I unfastened my bra and let it fall to the floor. He took a deep breath and I watched the torment in his eyes.

This was easy.

"It's okay, you can look" I said, innocently.

"You play dirty."

"Just how you like it."

"You know me so well." He grinned before taking his T-shirt off. When I heard him unfasten the zip on his jeans, I knew that my chances of winning our little game had just rapidly decreased.

"Well...I've taken my pants off" he announced.

"Good for you."

He smirked, "It'll be even better for you, I'll make sure of it."

My brain was screaming at me to look down but my stubbornness was winning. For now.

"You should probably take yours off too."

"I wasn't wearing any to begin with" I replied.

His eyes widened and I couldn't help but laugh. "You are one tough cookie, April Adams."

"Go ahead, take a bite."

When I heard him unscrew the lid to the body paint, I knew that I wouldn't be able to last much longer. "Now who's playing dirty?" I asked.

"Baby, I'm only just getting started."

The next thing I knew, something wet was dripping down the full length of my body. "Wow, is that all it takes?" I asked, sarcastically.

He smiled, "It's not my fault that you're so sexy."

I raised my eyebrow as I took hold of his hands and placed them against my breasts. I began to move them in slow circles, spreading the chocolate all over. I moaned, "Mmmmm, that feels so good."

He growled before conceding and looking down.

I let go of his hands, "I win!"

"In about ten seconds, you're going to be flat on your back while I lick every inch of your body clean. If anyone's a winner, it's me."

"We should play this game more often" I said as he threw me over his shoulder and carried me into the bedroom.

***

I sighed as I laid my head against his bare chest, "I wish I could stay the night."

"Then stay, we've still got half a tub of chocolate body paint left."

I laughed, "I don't want Brody to come over and kick your ass."

"He was cool about us when he came to see me."

I jumped up, "What? When?"

He grinned, "Don't look so worried. He came to see me this morning and we had a long chat."

"And?"

"And nothing. He's cool about it, he wants it to work out for us. We shook hands and everything." He smiled proudly, "I think he likes me."

"In that case, I'm staying the night. Why didn't you tell me before?"

"We were too busy with the chocolate."

An hour later, the rest of the body paint was gone.

Chapter Fifteen

I opened my eyes to see Isaac sat up in bed, reading. He must have been able to sense me looking at him because he grinned before turning to face me, "Good morning, gorgeous."

"Good morning, what are you reading?"

His eyes twinkled before he lifted up the book to show me. I sat up at lightning speed, "*Beautiful Disaster?*"

He shrugged, "I wanted to see what all of the fuss was about. You keep harping on about this Travis guy, I need to see who I'm up against."

Beautiful Disaster was my favourite book.

Isaac was my favourite person.

Put them together and it felt like *I* was in a novel.

A fantasy novel.

"When did you buy it?"

"A couple of days ago. I knew that it was one of your favourites so I wanted to replace it for you."

"You're the best boyfriend ever. How did you even remember what it was called?"

"I'm an awesome boyfriend with an awesome memory. And I might have had a little look on your Goodreads account."

My mouth dropped open, "You know what Goodreads is?"

He grinned, "*Of course* I know what it is."

"This just keeps getting better and better. So what are your thoughts on the book so far?" I laughed when he shrugged. "Are you jealous?"

He pouted, "No."

"Somebody's jealous" I sang. "You've got nothing to be jealous of, I love you way more than any book boyfriend."

"I should hope so, *they* can't cover you in chocolate body paint."

I took the book off him and placed it on the nightstand before climbing on top of him, "My reality is much better than any love story."

***

Isaac dropped me off at Lucy's on his way to work. I didn't have any classes for another hour so it gave me chance to get changed and pick my books up. I saw Brody's bike outside and wondered if he was going to be cool about me staying out last night. His text back had been short. I hung my coat up next to Lucy's before walking into the living room. Nobody was in there but I knew that someone was home because the shower was running. I went into my bedroom to get changed. Five minutes later, just as I was tying my converse, I heard a moan coming from the bathroom.

A female moan.

I opened my bedroom door and heard it again. There was definitely a woman in there. Just as I was about to go and investigate, Brody appeared, wearing only a towel. "Oh shit" he said, closing the door behind him.

I held my hand up and closed my eyes, "Please tell me that you haven't got a woman in there."

"I'm sorry, I didn't think you would be back until tonight. I thought you were going straight to class."

"Where's Lucy?"

"Um, she left about an hour ago."

"Brody, what were you thinking? This isn't our flat which means that you can't bring people here without asking Lucy first. You definitely can't have sex with random women in her shower. Are you trying to get us kicked out?"

"Of course not. I'm sorry, it won't happen again."

"You're damn right it won't." I nodded in the direction of the bathroom, "Tell her to get dressed and leave. If she's not gone in five minutes, I'm kicking her ass out."

He went to open the door but stopped and turned around, "Are you going to tell Lucy about this? I don't want it to be awkward."

"No, I won't tell her but if you ever bring somebody back here again, I'll kick you out myself."

He nodded before disappearing into the bathroom. I went back into my bedroom until I heard the front door open and close. I gave it another five minutes just to be safe until I ventured outside. Brody was sitting on the sofa, tapping away on his phone.

"I'll see you tonight, I expect lasagne" I told him as I put my coat back on. I froze when a thought popped into my head. I could have sworn that Lucy's coat had been next to mine when Isaac dropped me off. Could it have been Lucy who was in the shower with him? I glanced back over at Brody, who was grinning from ear to ear. I wasn't sure if I actually wanted to know the answer.

***

I was the first person to arrive at my lecture, followed by Hollie.

"What are you doing here so early?" she asked as she sat down next to me.

"I could ask you the same thing."

"You could, but you haven't."

"Hi Hollie, what are you doing here so early?"

She smirked, "I'm eager to learn."

I rolled my eyes, "Yeah, me too."

"How's your hot brother?"

"What's wrong? Are you getting fed up of Dan already?"

"Why do you always answer my questions with another question?"

I smirked, "Do I?"

She sighed, "Dan is good for when I've ran out of batteries."

I laughed, "Wow, say it how it is..."

"I always do. So, is Brody single?"

"Yep, he's not the dating type."

"Neither am I. See, we're a perfect match."

The door opened and I looked up to see Lucy walking over to us. She grinned as she sat down, "Good morning."

"Good morning to you too. Somebody's in a good mood."

She shrugged, "It's nearly weekend."

I narrowed my eyes as she took off her coat. The coat which I could have sworn was hanging up next to mine before it had miraculously disappeared.

Hollie nudged me, "Speaking of which, will you ask him if he wants to go out for a drink?"

"Who are we talking about?" Lucy asked.

I rolled my eyes, "Hollie thinks that she's the perfect match for Brody."

"He doesn't date" Lucy replied, matter-of-factly.

"Nobody said anything about dating. I just want to have some fun and find out if the rumours are true."

"What rumours?" Lucy asked.

I held my hands up, "I don't want to know."

Hollie glanced at me before whispering something to Lucy. Her face fell as she sat back in her chair, "Where did you hear that?"

"Where do you think?"

"I don't know, that's why I'm asking you" she snapped.

"Facebook, *obviously*. I learn more on there than I do in class. Brody's pretty popular at the minute, he's plastered all over girls walls."

"Um, can we please stop talking about my brother? It's weird."

Hollie laughed, "Okay, just one more question..." she turned to Lucy, "Has he really got an eight pack?" When Lucy ignored her, she carried on, "He's staying at your place, are you trying to tell me that you haven't seen him without a shirt on? Missed opportunity my friend, missed opportunity."

"I'm still here and it's still weird" I added.

Hollie laughed, "Okay, I guess I'll just have to find out for myself."

***

As soon as the lecture ended, Lucy darted out of the hall.

"Hey, are you okay?" I asked when I finally caught up to her.

She shrugged, "I'm fine."

Maybe Isaac was right about that word, she didn't look *fine*. Her good mood had completely vanished. "What was with the speedy exit?"

"I don't want to be late for my next class."

"Did Hollie say something to upset you earlier?"

"It's got nothing to do with me."

She picked up the pace and I was almost running to keep up with her. I gently took hold of her arm, "What's wrong?"

She stopped and turned to face me, "Why didn't you tell me that he's a Dad?"

"Who?" I asked, completely confused.

"Brody."

"What are you talking about?"

"Hollie told me that he got somebody called Leah pregnant and she gave birth last week."

I shook my head, "That's a lie, he would have told me."

"Why did he come to visit you?"

"Is that some kind of trick question?"

"Don't you think the timing is strange? Some girl claims to have given birth to his kid and then he turns up here out of the blue?"

I took a step closer to her, "What are you trying to say?"

"I'm just telling you what I've heard, maybe you should talk to him about it."

"Maybe *you* should talk to him about it. Why are you so upset over a stupid rumour?"

She blushed, "I saw a different side to him last night...one that I liked. He dropped the whole bad boy act and was just himself. We talked for hours and then this morning..." She shrugged, "It felt like we were making progress, that's all. It would have been nice of him to mention it to me if it's true."

"Well it's not true. End of story."

"I'd better go, I don't want to be late for class."

As I watched her walk away, my gut instinct was telling me that something had happened between them. I just hoped that she knew what she was getting herself in to.

Chapter Sixteen

I finished the rest of my classes and got back to Lucy's to find Brody sitting at the kitchen table. His leg was bouncing up and down like it does whenever he's nervous.

"Hey, are you okay?" I asked.

"April, will you sit down? I have something to tell you."

A knot formed in my stomach, "Oh my god, are the rumours true?"

"What? Has it already got out?"

"I didn't believe it, I thought it was a lie."

"Thanks for the vote of confidence."

"How could you?"

His face fell, "What? Are you not happy for me?"

"Honestly? No, I'm not. I don't think you're ready for it, you're too young."

"What does age have to do with it? I've wanted this for a long time, you know that."

"Since when?"

"Since I was a kid."

"Why didn't you tell me before now?"

"I only found out today."

I sat down and took a deep breath, "I can't believe that I'm an auntie."

"What are you talking about?"

"Your baby! I don't even know what it's called. Is it a boy or a girl?"

He jumped up, "What the fuck are you talking about? You're scaring me now."

"Wait, I thought that's what we've just been talking about..."

"I sure as shit wasn't talking about any baby." He held his hands up, "I'm always careful. Every single time."

"There are rumours going around that you got some girl called Leah pregnant."

He started laughing, "Oh my god and you thought it was true. I wondered why you were being such a bitch."

"Hang on, so it's not true?"

He took a few deep breaths and managed to stop laughing, "No, Leah is some psycho groupie. She wanted to have sex with me but I said no. I've never even touched her. A couple of weeks later, she got pregnant and told everybody that it was my kid. I've even taken a DNA test to prove that it's not mine."

"Oh thank god, so you're not a complete idiot after all."

"Have a little faith."

"Well what was I supposed to think? You were acting all nervous and then you said that you wanted to talk to me about something."

"I do, I have some awesome news."

I placed my hand over my heart, "I don't know if I can take any more."

A huge grin spread across his face, "Well you're going to have to because you're looking at a signed artist."

"What?"

"The band! We've been signed!"

We both started jumping up and down. "Oh my god! Are you being serious?"

"Deadly fucking serious" he replied as he picked me up and spun me around.

I half laughed, half screamed, "Congratulations! I'm so proud of you!" My head was spinning when he placed me back down, "Oh my god, my brother is going to be a rock star! Tell me everything!"

I knew that I would remember this moment for the rest of my life. The moment when my brother's life was about to change forever. One day, I would sit my grandchildren down and tell them all about this moment.

"I got the call about an hour ago, they want us to fly to America to meet with the record company and lay down some test tracks."

"That's awesome, when are you going?"

"Saturday."

"Woah, that's only two days away."

"I know, they said that we could be there for a couple of months. They're paying for a private villa and everything."

"I'm definitely coming to visit you, you can fly me out in the record labels private jet."

He chuckled, "Hell yes, only the best for my little sister. I still can't believe it. I mean, we're getting signed to the same record company as the D-Bags and The Mighty Storm. How fucking awesome is that?"

I stood up, "Oh. My. God. You're going to meet Kellan Kyle! Will you get me his autograph?"

"Why do you need his autograph when you can have mine?"

I raised my eyebrow, "Dude, it's Kellan Kyle."

"This isn't real."

"It *is* real and you deserve it, I'm so happy for you." His mood seemed to darken. "Hey, what's wrong?"

"I'm just worried about leaving people behind."

I sighed, "If you're talking about Mum then stop worrying. She's forty eight years old, it's about time she looked after herself. Don't you dare feel guilty, you've already sacrificed too much for her. This is your time to shine."

"When did you get so wise?"

"The day I was born."

He laughed as he pulled me into a giant hug. "I'm actually going to miss this place, no wonder students are willing to get into so much debt to come here."

I heard the front door close and turned around to see Lucy watching us. She smiled before heading towards her bedroom.

"Lucy, wait..." Brody shouted.

"No, I don't want to interrupt."

"You're not, I have some good news."

She stopped walking, "I've already heard, congratulations."

"The rumours aren't true" he replied.

She turned around to face us, "It's not your baby?"

"No, she made it all up. I even took a DNA test to prove it."

"So then, what's the good news?"

"The band have been signed."

"Oh my god!" Her face lit up as she ran over to him and threw her arms around his neck.

I slipped away unnoticed. I didn't need to ask if something was happening between them. I already knew the answer.

Chapter Seventeen

After classes on Thursday, I went shopping before heading over to Isaac's. I wanted to give Lucy and Brody some time alone.

I turned up wearing my newly bought trench coat and killer heels. "I have something for you" I told him as I led him over to the sofa. I sat him down before shaking my hair free from its ponytail. His eyes turned fiery as I very slowly began to untie my belt. He looked like he was about to pounce any minute. Finally, I let my coat drop to the floor to reveal my Team Isaac T-shirt.

He chuckled, "That is the best T-shirt that I have ever seen."

I held my hand up when he went to stand, "Sit down." He raised his eyebrow in question but did as he was told. "It's what's underneath that counts, remember?"

He bit his lip which made me want to do it. I walked towards him and slowly lowered myself onto his lap before taking off my T-shirt. I felt his erection press against my thigh as he took in the sight of my red, lace bra. His eyes slowly made their way down to my shorts, "Are you matching?"

I shrugged, "You'll have to find out for yourself." His eyes turned dark. "Maybe I've gone commando."

He stood up and wrapped my legs around his waist. He carried me into the kitchen before placing me on top of the counter. "You know that I love you, don't you?"

"Yes..."

"Good because I'm not going to make love to you. I'm going to fuck you so hard that you won't be able to think or walk straight afterwards." His eyes widened as he pulled off my shorts, "Holy shit, I thought you were teasing about going commando."

Chapter Eighteen

On Friday night, we decided to go out to celebrate Brody's news. Lucy and Brody went out for something to eat first, giving me a couple of hours to kill. I quite enjoyed having some time alone, it was one of the things that I missed about not having my own place. I decided to make a start on some coursework.

About an hour later, my phone rang. I grinned when I saw Isaac's name flash across the screen. "Hey beautiful" he purred, "What are you doing?"

"This really exciting thing called coursework. I thought it was a good idea to start it while I've got the house to myself. What about you?"

"I'm driving home from work. Where are the others?"

"They've gone out to line their stomachs."

He laughed, "Well I'm gonna go, I don't want to distract you from your work. I'll call you later."

I allowed myself five minutes to daydream about him before carrying on with my work. Not long after, there was a knock at the door.

"I'm coming" I shouted.

"You will be in about ten minutes" Isaac replied when I opened the door.

I grinned as my stomach did a somersault, "Prove it."

I knew that it was risky having him here but I doubted Lucy or Brody would be home any time soon. Plus, the added element of danger turned me on. I questioned whether I was being a hypocrite after I scolded Brody for bringing somebody back here. But that thought was quickly disregarded and replaced by the thought of getting Isaac naked. I pulled him inside and locked the door behind us.

"How brave are you feeling?" he asked before lifting me up. I could feel how much he wanted me. He carried me into the kitchen and placed me on top of the counter.

"Have you got a death wish? What if my brother walks in on us?"

"What if he doesn't?"

I shook my head, "There's a fine line between being brave and being stupid. Bedroom, now."

He laughed, "I love it when you're bossy. Which room is yours?"

"The one with the door open."

I was flat on my back in less than ten seconds. I watched him take off his T-shirt before starting on his jeans. My eyes roamed his perfectly toned body.

He laughed, "Are you just going to lie there and drool?"

I placed my hands behind my head, "Yep, why have you stopped?"

"I was waiting for the stripper music to kick in." He grinned before taking off his jeans, "Like what you see?" I nodded as I pulled him on top of me. "You know, I was thinking about having a little cardio workout tonight. Maybe you could help me?"

"I would love to."

He began to unbutton my jeans, "You're going to get very sweaty, I think we should take these off." I lifted my hips up, allowing him to pull them off.

"So you probably won't be needing these?" I asked as I pulled down his boxer shorts. "I think we should start our warm up."

I froze when I heard the front door open. "Shit, shit, shit" I whispered as I jumped up and began to pick up our clothes off the floor. Why were they back so early?

I had to bite my lip to stop myself from laughing when I watched Isaac attempt to hide in the wardrobe. "Seriously? That only happens in movies."

"April? We're back" Lucy shouted.

"Okay, just a second" I replied as I handed Isaac his clothes and slipped into my dressing gown. "Stay here."

"As opposed to what? Going out there with you? Oh hey Lucy, how's it going?"

"Very funny." I took a step towards the door but he pulled me back and gave me a full on Hollywood kiss which left me breathless. I took a moment to gather my thoughts before opening the door.

Lucy laughed, "Hey, is that your outfit for tonight?"

I closed the door behind me before looking down at my fluffy dressing down, "Um, no, I've just been in the shower. How was the food?"

Brody narrowed his eyes, "Your hair isn't wet."

"I have this thing called a hair dryer. So, how was the food?"

"It was tasty" Lucy replied.

"Good, you're back early."

"Yeah, the service was really quick."

"Awesome."

Brody stood up and looked out of the window. A few seconds later, he turned around to face us, "How long will it take you two to get ready? It's time to get the party started."

"Not long, I just need to finish something off."

He raised his eyebrow, "Finish something off? *Really?*"

I frowned, "Yeah, I've been working on some coursework."

"Coursework? Is that what you call it?"

I pointed to the table where my papers and books were spread out, "Yes."

Lucy laughed, "I'm going to get changed."

I waited until she closed her bedroom door before rushing over to Brody, "What are you playing at?" I whispered.

"Isaac's left so you may as well get dressed so we can go out."

"Wait, what?"

"I watched him walk down the street about twenty seconds ago." He winked, "Good job we're on the first floor."

I rushed back into my bedroom, which was now empty. I even checked inside the wardrobe like a loser. Brody was telling the truth, Isaac was gone. I looked out of the window but there was no sign of him. I sent him a text message -

"Was it something I said?"

"I was unimpressed by the lack of wardrobe space."

"Tell me the truth...are you really in Narnia right now?"

"Yes, I have an awesome signal over here."

"I knew it! I'll call you later. P.S. You owe me a workout."

"I think we should work out twice a day from now on."

"Deal!!!"

I was about to get dressed when I saw a note on my pillow. I unfolded it and smiled when I saw that it was one of Isaac's diary entries -

<u>What I've learned...</u>

Her name is April.

She likes my lanterns.

Red lipstick is hot.

Mixers don't suck after all.

I like dancing.

I hate sharing.

She makes me happy.

Chapter Nineteen

An hour later, I was already tipsy. I was the definition of a lightweight.

"A toast" I announced as I raised my glass, "To big brothers and record deals."

Brody grinned from ear to ear, "And to awesome little sisters."

"Cheers to that." We clinked our glasses and took a drink before he went straight back to watching Lucy. She was stood at the bar talking to some people from her class but kept glancing over at us. I laughed, "You're staring."

He raised his eyebrow before turning to face me, "Do you ever worry that I'll forget about you once I'm famous?"

"Nope."

"Well you should."

I punched his arm, which probably hurt my hand more than it hurt him. "Do you ever worry that I'll sell embarrassing stories about you?"

He winked, "Any press is good press."

"I have a question for you."

"For the millionth time, I don't know why I got the looks and you got the brains."

I rolled my eyes, "I'm trying to be serious here." He put on his best serious face which just made me giggle. "Look, I don't know what's happening between you and Lucy and you don't have to tell me. Lord knows that I haven't got a leg to stand on but you're leaving soon, will I be left to pick up the pieces?"

"What are you asking me?"

"Is she going to be okay when you're gone?"

"Of course."

"Please don't break her heart."

"Are you going to have this conversation with her too? Are you going to warn her not to break mine?"

I narrowed my eyes, "Do I need to warn her?"

She was on her way back to us before he could answer.

***

"I like drunk April" Lucy shouted as we stood at the bar.

"And I like tequila! Two tequilas please."

"Sure thing" the bartender replied before pouring the shots. He winked, "They're on the house."

I downed it, "Thanks."

"Tough day?" he asked as I winced.

"Tough life."

Lucy giggled, "Drama queen."

"Hey! My house burnt down!"

"Maybe you could tell me all about it later?" The bartender asked, "I finish at two thirty."

"Thanks but no thanks" I replied as I dragged Lucy away from the bar.

"What's wrong with you? He's hot!"

"I'm not interested."

"Why not? Are you still into Lukas?"

"No, we're just friends."

"Then why aren't you interested?"

He's not Isaac.

"He's not my type."

"Are you a lesbian?"

"Yep, I burnt my own house down so I could live with you and spy on you when you take a shower."

"I knew it!" she shouted.

"And now I'm about to dry hump your leg on the dance floor."

***

We went to a few more bars before hitting a club. We met up with some of Lucy's friends who had no shame in hiding their feelings for Brody. As soon as he went to get more drinks, the locker talk began.

"He is one hot piece of ass."

"Oh, the things I would do to him."

"April, your brother is coming home with me tonight."

That last comment earned a dirty look from Lucy.

"Awesome" I muttered.

"What?" Lucy asked, looking unimpressed with her friends.

"Douchebag alert" I pointed to Dan and Hollie.

"Did you invite them?"

"Nope."

"Well let's just hope that they don't see us."

I sighed, "Too late, they're coming over."

"Ladies, the party has arrived!" Dan announced.

I ignored him and smiled at Hollie, "Hey."

"Hey, what are you two doing here?" she asked.

"Celebrating."

"Oooh, what's the occasion?"

"Brody's band has been signed."

Dan lost interest and began to flirt with some of Lucy's friends.

"That's awesome, I'll have to congratulate him."

I heard Lucy mutter something under her breath.

"I know, it's the same record company as the D-Bags. I can't stop name dropping."

"Woah, can he get me Griffin's number?"

Griffin. Typical.

"Who the fuck is Gryffindor?" Dan asked, suddenly interested in our conversation again.

I rolled my eyes, "Gryffindor is a house in Harry Potter. *Griffin* is a badass musician."

"Whatever, I'm going to get a drink."

I leaned closer to him, "Just a heads up, I'd stay away from Brody if I were you. He's stopped taking his meds."

His eyes widened, "Meds?"

"Yeah, he's a little unstable right now."

"That explains the other night."

I nodded, trying my best not to laugh as he walked away. At least now he might keep his distance. Brody came back with our drinks a few minutes later.

"Congratulations, sugar" Hollie said before planting a kiss on his lips.

He wiped his mouth with the back of his hand before glancing at Lucy.

"I'll be right back" she announced.

"Are you okay?" I asked.

"Yep, just going to the Ladies."

"Oh, I'll come with you before I find Dan" Hollie added.

Lucy sighed before walking away.

Brody downed his drink before starting on another one, "You better keep Dan away from me tonight."

"Why do you hate him so much?"

He raised his eyebrow before pointing to the bar. Dan had his hands all over two random girls. "There's your answer."

I laughed, "I get that he's a dick but it's like you can't even stand to be in the same room as him."

"Um, what does it look like I'm doing right now?"

"Having a staring contest with him" I leaned in closer, "But it only counts if the other person is looking."

"I don't like how he treats women." He cleared his throat when I finally stopped laughing, "What's so funny?"

"Oh come on! Pot meet kettle."

He scowled, "No, I am *nothing* like him. I don't hurt people."

I had a feeling that he knew more than he was letting on. "Do you know something that I don't?"

"Lucy told me a few things last night. He was a complete dickhead to her the other day."

"When?"

"She said they were at the pub and he got wasted. He's lucky that I haven't knocked him out."

"Yeah well keep it that way, maybe we should go to another club to keep you out of trouble."

Brody raised his empty glass, "Or maybe we should have another drink."

Chapter Twenty

One hour and two glasses of wine later, I was in a taxi on my way to Isaac's. Brody kept insisting that he didn't want me to leave on my own so I took him to the side and explained that I wasn't going back to Lucy's.

I knew that I was taking a risk by coming here when the bar was still open but I was too drunk and horny to care. I asked the taxi driver to drop me off around the back. I punched the code into the door and then opened it an inch to check that nobody was there. When the coast was clear, I ran inside and straight up the stairs to his apartment. I started to panic when he didn't answer. Maybe I should have called to check that he was home first. What if somebody saw me up here? How would I explain getting past the bar? I crossed my fingers and knocked again. I felt a huge sense of relief when I heard his voice, "Just a minute" he shouted.

I flattened my dress down and leaned against the doorframe, trying my best to look seductive. When I realised that I just looked like an idiot, I straightened up. My whole body cried out for him when he opened the door wearing only a towel. A drop of water fell from his hair onto his chest before making its way down the ridges of his six pack. "What a nice surprise" he purred.

"I think that should be my line." I stepped inside before closing the door behind me. "Drop the towel."

He smirked, "Seeing as though you asked so nicely..." It soon became clear that I wasn't the only one who was turned on. I lowered myself to my knees. "Is this a dream?" he asked as I gazed up at him.

"I don't know, does this happen in your dreams?" He growled when I began to tease him with the tip of my tongue. "What happens next?"

"You open your sweet little mouth."

"There's nothing sweet about what I'm about to do."

I paused when his house phone began to ring.

"Don't stop, baby. Do you know how much it turns me on, seeing you on your knees?"

I shook my head innocently before taking him in my mouth. He threw his head back and I moaned at how good he tasted. His phone carried on ringing until the answer machine picked it up. The sound of Abbie's voice filled the room, completely killing my mood. Why was she calling him this late at night? I stopped and looked up at him questioningly.

He held his hand out to me, "Come on, I need you in my bed." I took his hand but something that Abbie said caught my attention. He wrapped his arms around my waist and began to kiss my neck, "Your lips are perfect. So soft, so sexy."

I pulled away, alarmed at what Abbie was now saying - *"Are you going to tell her?"*

Isaac tried to lead me to his room but I let go of his hand. I turned around and walked over to the answer machine.

"Just ignore her" he said.

Abbie carried on, *"Do you want to make a fool out of her?"*

The adrenaline began pumping through my veins. Isaac was about to pick up the phone when I held my arm out, "Don't you dare."

"She's not going to be happy when she finds out our little secret..."

I felt sick. My gut was telling me that something bad was about to happen. Was I the one who was dreaming? Was this a nightmare?

"Do you think that innocent little April is going to stay with you when I tell her?" She laughed, *"Actually, I don't need to tell her, I can just show her."*

My heart stopped when I heard her say the words that I knew would haunt me forever - *"Do you think that she's still going to love you when I show everybody the tape? You can stop this now before she finds out, before she gets hurt."*

I couldn't listen to any more. I turned and ran straight out of the door. Isaac followed me down the stairs but must have realised that he wasn't wearing any clothes. I didn't stop running until I was inside the petrol station opposite the bar. I bent down, trying to catch my breath.

"Are you okay?" The cashier asked, looking concerned.

Don't cry, don't cry, don't cry.

"I'm fine" I replied, my voice shaky.

"Were you running away from someone?"

"No, it's just cold outside." I pulled my phone out of my bag and ordered a taxi. After cancelling Isaac's incoming call, I rang Brody. "Something's happened, I'll be at Lucy's in ten minutes."

"Are you okay?"

"No."

"Has Isaac done something?"

"Yes, I'll explain when I see you."

"I'm getting a taxi back to Lucy's now."

"Okay. Brody? Don't let him near me."

I turned my phone off, ignoring the voicemails from Isaac.

When I got into the taxi a few minutes later, I looked over and saw that his car was gone. Was he out looking for me or had he gone to see Abbie?

Chapter Twenty One

I'm not sure which one woke me up first, the pounding in my head or the barbed wire in my throat. I had the hangover from hell. I ached all over, it even hurt to blink. I made a vow to never drink again. Then I made a vow to stop lying to myself.

After a good few minutes of feeling sorry for myself, my heart broke all over again when I remembered what had happened last night. The physical pain in my chest was way worse than any hangover. I would rather have a hangover every single day for the rest of my life than feel this kind of pain.

I turned over and nearly had a full on heart attack when I saw Isaac sitting in front of the bedroom door. I sat up way too fast and immediately regretted it. I allowed the dizziness to subside before I took a proper look at him. He looked exhausted. I was about to shout for Brody when I remembered where I was. Regardless of what happened last night, Lucy couldn't know that Isaac was here.

"What are you doing here?"

"Brody let me in."

Traitor.

"Why? I told him to keep you away from me."

"I know but I need to talk to you."

"Talk to me or hold me hostage?"

"Whatever it takes for you to listen to me."

"The damage has already been done."

"April, I swear that nothing happened between me and Abbie."

"Save your breath, I heard what she said on the answer machine."

"Yes and you didn't give me a chance to explain. Instead you jumped to conclusions and ran away."

"What was I supposed to think?"

"You were supposed to think that she's a lying bitch and I'm your boyfriend who you trust."

"You have five minutes to explain."

He sighed, "Remember when my mum rang me on the way back from the lake house?" I nodded. "Well she wanted me to go and pick Abbie up from the police station. She was questioned about the fire."

"Because of what I told them? About our disagreement?"

"Well that's what I thought until I found out she called Lukas on the day of the fire, asking what number house you lived at."

"What? Why would she do that?"

"She made up a story, said she wanted to go and talk to you about something."

"How do you know?"

"Lukas told me, I went to see him on the day that he got out of hospital."

I frowned. That was the same day that *I* went to visit him. My thoughts drifted back to when I was walking down his street and saw a car similar to Isaac's. Could that have been him? I remembered the phone call where Isaac had been acting strange. He said that he was busy and couldn't talk. Was that because he had been with Lukas at the time?

He stroked my hand, "It's okay, I know you went to see him too. You arrived just after I left."

I couldn't help but feel guilty. He knew that I went to see him all along but hadn't asked me about it. He must have thought that I was keeping it a secret. "I'm sorry, I didn't want to tell you over the phone and then Brody turned up and it just didn't come up. I know how it looks but I didn't keep it from you on purpose."

"I know you didn't. I'm sorry for keeping things from you too but I wanted to protect you. After seeing Lukas, I asked Abbie to tell me the truth but she swore that she had nothing to do with the fire. Of course, I didn't believe her but I didn't want to get on her bad side. A couple of days ago, she turned up at my place, a total mess. The police had interviewed her boyfriend, who told them that he wasn't with her the night of the fire. He was supposed to be her alibi." My mind was racing as he took a deep breath, "That's when it all started."

"When what started?"

"The blackmail. She wanted me to tell the police that I was with her before the fire, before I gave you a ride to your house. She wanted me to lie to them. That's when I knew that she did it."

I felt like I was going to throw up as the reality of what he was saying kicked in. "She set my house on fire?"

"Yes."

"Why didn't you tell me? Why didn't you tell the *police*?"

"April...she had a tape." Her words from last night started running through my head. "She had a tape of me and you. She threatened to show everybody including the University if I didn't help her."

I shook my head, "But how? What kind of tape?"

He placed his head in his hands, "The stockroom."

I shook my head, "No..."

"I'm so sorry."

I took a couple of deep breaths, "So you had CCTV in the stockroom and you let us do *that*?"

"Some stock went missing a few months ago so we installed a camera in there. I completely forgot about it. I didn't know that she checked the tapes."

"So she burnt my house down because she was jealous? She nearly killed Lukas because she saw us in the stockroom together?"

He didn't say anything. He didn't need to. I didn't know whether to scream or cry. "We need to tell the police."

He pulled something out of his pocket. I stood up and took a step closer to him, "What's that?"

He pushed a button and Abbie's voice filled the room, *"What do you want me to say, Isaac? I've already said that I'm sorry. I'm so fucking sorry for burning April's house down. What more do you want me to say?"*

"I want you to tell me why you did it" Isaac asked.

"I've already lost Sienna, I can't lose you too."

"Abbie, you nearly killed an innocent person. Lukas nearly died because of you."

"I didn't know he was going to turn all knight in shining armour, did I? I didn't know that he loved her that much."

"Did you think that April was in the house?"

My heart stopped as I waited to hear her response. After a long silence, she began to cry, *"Please don't hate me, Isaac. You* know that I'm not a bad person deep down. I had a lot to drink and I wasn't thinking straight."

"Answer the question."

There was another long pause.

"Yes, I thought she was in the house."

My legs gave way as I began to sob quietly. Thank god that I wasn't in the house. Isaac sat down next to me and pulled me into his arms. We stayed like that for a while until I managed to calm down. "I want to hear the rest."

"Are you sure?"

I nodded so he pressed play.

"Why are you blackmailing me?" he asked Abbie.

"Because you've left me no choice. I wouldn't have to blackmail you if you actually wanted to help me. After everything that we've been through, you should want to help me."

"What would you want me to tell the Police?"

"Tell them that I was with you the night of the fire. I don't care about the details, make something up."

"So you want me to lie, even though I didn't see you at all that night?"

"Yes."

"And what if I say no?"

"Then I'll release the tape. Trust me, it's not going to look good on April's CV."

The recording ended.

"About twenty minutes after that, she was arrested for arson and attempted murder." My whole body was shaking. "I won't let anybody come close to hurting you ever again. I will spend the rest of my life making sure that you're safe and happy if you'll let me. I know that I haven't been acting myself lately but I didn't want to involve you. You've already been through so much, I didn't want to put any more stress on you. I knew that I couldn't let her release that tape. We've come so far and I wasn't going to let her ruin it all for us, ruin your chances of getting the career that you want. I'm sorry for keeping things from you."

I shook my head, "Isaac, you don't need to apologise. I should be the one apologising. I'm so sorry for doubting you last night, I feel like such a fool. You were trying to do the right thing and I was too busy jumping to conclusions."

"Look at me. We were *both* fools. I should have told you everything from the start. From now on, we need to be completely honest with each other. We're a team. Good or bad, we will work things out together. We need to focus on our future. Abbie's going to prison for a very long time."

"What about the tape?"

"I have it."

"How?"

"I took it from her apartment before the police arrived."

I shook my head, trying to process everything. "How did you persuade Brody to let you in here?"

"I told him everything...after he finished pushing me up against the wall."

"Does Lucy know that you're here?"

He nodded, "She was with Brody the whole time, I didn't know what else to do."

"So she knows?"

"She knows that I'm more than just your tutor but she doesn't know everything."

I took a deep breath, "I can't believe it." He held me in his arms for a long time before we finally left the room.

Brody and Lucy were sitting on the sofa. He stood up when he saw me. "Is everything okay?"

I nodded.

"How are you feeling?" Lucy asked.

"Like I've been run over...several times."

She stood up, "That's tequila for you. Do you want us to go out and get some breakfast? Give you two some time alone?"

"No, I want you to stay." I turned to Brody, "What time are you leaving?"

"In about an hour but there's been a change of plan. Isaac's giving me a ride home instead. I'm keeping my bike at the bar while I'm away."

"Why?"

"So Isaac can ride the death trap. He may as well get some use out of it..."

My eyes snapped to Isaac's. He laughed, "Calm down, I'm not as cool as your brother."

"Sis, do you really think that I want to leave my bike at home? Mum would probably sell it to buy more booze."

"I'm going to make pancakes" Lucy announced.

"I'll help" Isaac added before following her into the kitchen.

I turned to face Brody, "Are you sure it's a good idea to let Isaac take you home? What about Mum?"

He wrapped his arm around my shoulders, "Don't worry, she's still in rehab."

"Then I'm coming too."

Chapter Twenty Two

An hour later, we were full of pancakes and on our way. Lucy had tears in her eyes as she said goodbye to Brody but insisted that she didn't want me to stay at home with her. I think she needed some time alone. I noticed that she was wearing Brody's ring on a chain around her neck.

Isaac and Brody spent the whole journey talking about music and I was quite content listening to them. It made me happy that my two favourite guys in the entire world seemed to genuinely like each other.

"It's the second house on the right" Brody announced as we turned onto our street. It felt strange being back, so much had happened since leaving a few months ago. Isaac parked up before shaking Brody's hand, "It's been a pleasure."

I laughed, "Sweet talker."

"There's nothing wrong with a bit of bromance" Brody winked, "Make sure you treat my little sister right or I'll set my psycho groupies on you."

"You can keep them all to yourself" Isaac replied, laughing.

"Go and show America what you've got!" I told Brody as we got out of the car and I pulled him into a giant hug. I was going to miss having him around but I knew that he was leaving for bigger and better things.

"I will. Be careful and call me any time you want."

"You're going to regret saying that. Different time zones, remember?"

"Okay, just stick to mornings."

"My mornings on your mornings?"

He laughed, "You know what? I'll call you. Look after Lucy for me, okay?"

I nodded but his face turned serious, "Hey, don't worry, she'll be fine."

"Shit."

"What's wrong?"

"She shouldn't be back yet."

"Who?" I turned around and quickly discovered who he was talking about. The front door opened and out walked my mother.

I didn't know whether to talk to her or get back in the car and tell Isaac to drive away. She made the choice for me when she walked over to us. She didn't fall over, which was a good start. She pulled me into her arms, "It's so nice to see you." I was surprised when she didn't reek of alcohol. "I've missed both of you." She turned to Brody, "I didn't think you were coming back."

He shook his head, "I'm not staying, why don't we go inside and talk?"

"Who's that?" she asked, looking at Isaac.

Before I could stop him, he got out of the car and extended his hand, "Hi, I'm Isaac. It's nice to meet you."

"We should be heading back" I said as they shook hands. I didn't want my mum to embarrass me in front of Isaac.

"Are you still coming home for Christmas?" she asked.

I shrugged, "Are you going to be sober by Christmas"

"I hope so."

"Me too."

I said goodbye and hugged Brody one more time before getting back in the car.

"Are you okay?" Isaac asked as we drove away.

"I'm fine."

"You really need to learn some new adjectives."

I rolled my eyes, "*Fine*, maybe I will."

He laughed. When we pulled up at some traffic lights, he turned to face me, "Why don't you ever talk about her?"

"There's nothing to say. She's an alcoholic, end of story."

"I don't think it has to be the end, I know someone who could help her."

"Are they a miracle worker?"

"No but they're really good at what they do."

"Isaac, you don't have to help her."

"You're right, I don't *have* to help her but I *want* to."

I glanced out of the window, scared of letting my two worlds collide. I wanted to keep my life with Isaac separate from my mother but I had a strong feeling that it was out of my hands.

"Can we make one more stop before we head back?"

He grinned, "Of course."

***

After squealing in our faces for five minutes, we brought Katie up to date with everything that had happened.

"Oh my god! My best friend is a fucking porn star!" Katie whispered after she dragged me into the kitchen, leaving Isaac in the living room with Ian and Jamie.

"I knew I shouldn't have told you."

"Can I have a signed copy?"

"You've got serious mental issues."

"Hey, I'm not the one who made a sex tape." She pulled her phone out of her pocket, "I'm googling it right now."

"You're not going to find it."

"Well that's weird because it's already buffering."

"What?!"

"Yeah, it's right here on WWW dot my best friend is a porn star and made a sex tape with her hot tutor dot com." I had to listen to her laugh for two whole minutes.

"That's not funny."

"I disagree. Have you watched it back yet? You could totally self-evaluate."

"No and I'm not going to."

"You're such a spoil sport. So when are you going to make the next one?"

I sighed, "I'm so confused, I miss you but I don't at the same time..." Now it was my turn to laugh.

"You know, the whole student/teacher thing is popular in porn, you could draw from your real life experiences."

I only had myself to blame.

I quickly escaped before she could make any more porn related comments. I grinned when I saw Isaac bouncing Jamie on his knee.

"Oh my god, so he *can* be quiet" Katie said as she appeared next to me.

Ian chuckled, "You need to visit more often, he's not been this quiet in...forever."

She nudged me, "I'd keep this one if I were you."

I laughed, "That's the plan."

"Apparently his charm works on people of all ages." She winked at Isaac, "And genders."

We all burst out laughing.

Chapter Twenty Three

I walked into my lecture on Monday morning and grinned when I saw Lukas sitting in the front row. It had been weeks since we were in a class together. "Hey, stranger."

"Hey, I saved you a seat."

I sat down next to him, "Thanks. I haven't seen you in class for a while, have you been on holiday or something?"

He grinned, playing along with me, "Yes, actually."

"Did you go anywhere nice?"

"I went somewhere really hot." I burst out laughing but he carried on, "I went all inclusive. The food wasn't anything to write home about but they waited on me hand and foot."

"Well it's good to have you back."

"It's good to be back. How are things with you?"

"Great, thanks."

"Have you sorted your new accommodation out yet?"

I grinned, "Lucy asked me to be her official flatmate and I said yes."

"That's awesome."

I nodded, "We're having an official flat warming soon, you should come. It's nothing big, just close friends."

He grinned, "I like the sound of that."

"Me too."

I knew from that moment on that everything was going to be okay.

Chapter Twenty Four

The butterflies in my stomach came alive as I heard a key turning in the lock. Isaac's face lit up when he saw me, "Do you have any idea how awesome it is to come home and see your beautiful face in my apartment?"

I grinned as I walked over to him, "Not as awesome as this..." I threaded my hands through his hair as I leaned up to kiss him.

He set his briefcase down on the kitchen counter before picking me up. My legs naturally wrapped around his waist as he carried me into his bedroom. He placed me down on the bed and began to plant gentle kisses all over my face and neck, "Zero days."

I felt my eyes fill with tears, "We did it."

"We did it" he repeated.

"Is this real?"

"Hell yes, it's real. I've already changed my facebook status to in a relationship."

I giggled, "I love you."

"I love you too. So what do you want to do first? Feed each other ice cream or take selfies of us kissing?"

"Let's do both at the same time."

He grinned, "Deal."

Epilogue

Two years later

My heart swelled with pride as I looked out into the audience at all of my favourite people. Isaac was standing up taking photographs while my mum fussed over a heavily pregnant Katie. Brody slapped Ian on the back before waving at me.

Lukas nudged me, "Look how far we've come."

I let his words sink in as I turned to face him. I wanted to remember this moment forever. I was so grateful that we had managed to work through our problems. He would always be one of my best friends. "What a ride" I replied.

"Understatement of the century."

***

Half an hour later, I had officially graduated. Who knew that throwing a cap up in the air would feel so damn good? After being blinded by the flashes on everybody's cameras, we all headed back to the flat for the after-party.

"Speech!" Brody shouted as he tapped the side of his champagne glass.

I scowled at him. "I'm going to keep it short and sweet. I would just like to say a big thank you to everybody for coming. I'm so glad that I can share this special day with you all."

"Nice speech" Lucy told me once the clapping had died down.

"Thanks, you can do the next one."

She laughed before glancing over at Brody.

"He's been asking about you."

She blushed, "Who?"

"Oh, come on! You've just graduated, you can't get away with playing dumb."

A couple of months after Brody left for America the first time around, their phone calls stopped. To this day, both of them refuse to talk about what happened. She fiddled nervously with her necklace - the one which had Brody's ring on it. The one which she refused to take off. "I think you should talk to him."

She looked down at her feet, "I wouldn't even know where to start."

I caught Brody's eye and motioned for him to come over, "Start from the beginning."

Proving how perfectly attuned we were, Isaac came up and wrapped his arms around me before gently leading me away, leaving Lucy and Brody alone.

"I'm so proud of you."

I grinned, "I couldn't have done it without you."

"Will you come for a little walk with me?"

I wiggled my eyebrows, "A little walk, hmmm?"

He laughed, "Just a walk...for now."

"Do you think it's safe to leave those two alone?"

"Let's check." He shouted over to Brody, "Am I okay to steal your sister for a little while?"

"Sure, as long as you bring her back." Brody grinned at me as we walked out of the door.

I couldn't begin to get my head around how happy I was. Me and Isaac were the happiest we'd ever been, Brody's band was doing awesome and my mum was sober. Eighteen months and counting. I would never be able to thank Isaac enough for his compassion. After Brody left home, she spiralled out of control. Isaac paid for her to check into a private rehab centre. It was a long process but with the right help, she got her life back on track. I began visiting her once a month and we were slowly trying to patch up our relationship.

We strolled hand in hand until we arrived back at the University. "Why have you brought me back here? I've graduated, that's it, I'm free!"

He laughed, "I want to show you something."

"Oh yeah? I thought you said this was an innocent little walk?"

"April Adams, you have a dirty mind."

"Are you complaining?"

"Not one little bit."

When we reached the line of trees, he placed my hand on his bicep, "Hold on, I won't let you fall."

I laughed, "Wow, I feel like we've just been transported back in time. You know, I nearly died when you tensed your arm."

"When?"

"That first night at the mixer when you told me to hold on. You tensed your arm and I nearly melted onto the floor."

He winked, "I did it on purpose."

I gasped, "You did not!"

"I did, I wanted you to feel the guns."

We were both laughing when we reached our tree. I sighed happily as I ran my hand across the bark where the letters I and A were engraved. "I'm going to miss this place."

"Me too, we can come back and visit."

"I'd like that."

He wrapped his arms around my waist and gazed down at me, "I'm so glad that I came out here the morning that I met you."

"Well I'm glad that I was running late."

"Me too. Our relationship hasn't always been easy but I wouldn't change a thing. Everything happened the way that it did to lead us to this very moment." He reached into his pocket and pulled out a piece of folded up paper, "I have something for you."

I grinned, recognising the paper. I loved it when he shared his diary entries with me. It made me feel closer to him and it was a nice way of reflecting on the good times that we had shared. I took the paper from him and began to unfold it.

"You are the best thing that's ever happened to me."

I leaned up to kiss him, "Short but sweet, thank you." He handed me another one. "Two in one day? You're spoiling me!"

"I'm allowed to spoil you, it's your graduation day."

I grinned as I read his sweet words -

"I want to spend the rest of my life making you happy."

I laughed when I looked up to see that he was holding another one. His eyes twinkled as he handed it to me, "I've saved the best for last."

I unfolded the paper and gasped as I read his handwritten words -

"Will you marry me?"

My heart began to pound as he slowly got down on one knee. He reached into his jacket pocket and pulled out a small box. "April Adams, will you do me the honour of becoming my wife?"

I couldn't stop the tears from flowing as I threw my arms around him and nearly tackled him to the ground. "Yes! Of course I will marry you!" I felt like I was going to burst with happiness as he placed the ring on my finger. I looked around us, trying to absorb every little thing about this moment.

His eyes were brimming with tears as he gently wiped away mine, "Hey, what's with the April Showers?"

I took his hand and held it against my chest, "Feel that? It beats for you."

I grinned as I saw the next fifty years flash before my eyes. I saw love and happiness and grandchildren. *Lots* of grandchildren. I felt like the luckiest girl alive. Not only had I found my husband but I had found my best friend, my soul mate, my forever.

The End.

23896394R00085

Printed in Great Britain
by Amazon